"When did you g[...] Jason asked

"This morning," Sunny told him.

"Then take tomorrow and settle in. Friday's soon enough to poke around out here. Besides, I'd like a chance to prepare the men. I don't want any unnecessary alarms or false rumors spreading." Granted, he'd welcome the advice of a veterinarian, but the fact that the vet in question happened to be Sunny Carmichael bugged him. He needed to figure out why.

"Fine," she said. "I guess I'll have to trust your judgment about the urgency in this case."

"It's not a case, damn it."

He realized he was touchy. But it *was* his property, and she couldn't *make* him cooperate at this stage.

She was simply a veterinarian on vacation who was making a neighborly courtesy call.

Except, he was a man who had too many unresolved memories of Sunny Carmichael.

COURTED BY
A COWBOY
Mindy Neff

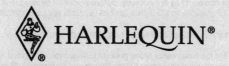

HARLEQUIN®

TORONTO • NEW YORK • LONDON
AMSTERDAM • PARIS • SYDNEY • HAMBURG
STOCKHOLM • ATHENS • TOKYO • MILAN • MADRID
PRAGUE • WARSAW • BUDAPEST • AUCKLAND

To wonderful new friends:
D'Ann Conner—for taking me under your wing
with a warm and generous heart.

And
Chriss Gerlach—for sharing your delightful animals
with me, especially the mare who can sleep through anything!

ISBN 0-373-16993-0

COURTED BY A COWBOY

Copyright © 2003 by Mindy Neff.

ABOUT THE AUTHOR

Originally from Louisiana, Mindy settled in Southern California, where she married a really romantic guy and raised five kids. Family, friends, writing and reading are her passions. When she's not writing, Mindy's ideal getaway is a good book, hot sunshine and a chair at the river's edge with water lapping at her toes.

Books by Mindy Neff

HARLEQUIN AMERICAN ROMANCE

Don't miss any of our special offers. Write to us at the following address for information on our newest releases.

Harlequin Reader Service
U.S.: 3010 Walden Ave., P.O. Box 1325, Buffalo, NY 14269
Canadian: P.O. Box 609, Fort Erie, Ont. L2A 5X3

Chapter One

If today had been a fish, Sunny Carmichael would've pitched it right back into the water.

She swept up the broken water glass and dumped it into the trash can, adding the clear shards to the shattered jelly jar already there. The jar's sticky contents lay smeared over the crumpled paper plates and napkins like a gooey mosaic decorating the den.

Putting away the broom, she noticed that her Doc Martens made sucking noises on the faux marble floor. *Oh, well,* she thought, sitting down at the kitchen table. She wasn't the greatest housecleaner. Animals were her forte.

Simba lumbered over and rested his huge head on her knee, looking up at her with velvety brown eyes that had snagged her the moment she'd seen him in the pound four years ago, surrounded by a litter of kittens. Part Labrador retriever, part Irish wolfhound, he was roughly the size of a month-old colt, with a tail that could knock a bull on his butt in one exuberant swoop, and a canine smile that apologized beforehand for his clumsiness.

"What's next, Simba? Mama says things break in

threes. We've had two in one day..." She patted
Simba's wide skull. "Three, if you count Michael."

Michael Lawrey had been her fiancé for the past
two years—until three days ago, when he'd dumped
her. Wealthy, passably handsome and powerful, he
was on a political climb with an eye toward the gov-
ernor's seat.

Evidently, he'd decided she no longer fit in with his
plans.

Sunny stared at the sticky floor, but couldn't work
up the energy to do anything about it. She was bored
and vaguely upset, when she should have been totally
torn up. After all, the man she was to marry had
chucked her. Something was wrong that she felt more
embarrassed and inadequate than heartbroken.

She wasn't sure what to do with herself. Here she
was on a beautiful summer Saturday evening, sitting
alone in a plush condo in Malibu, because not a soul
was willing to go out on the town with her.

Now that she wasn't part of a couple, she was per-
sona non grata in her and Michael's social circle.
Friends had chosen sides, and she'd been on the losing
one.

Finding herself all alone felt weird. The condo was
quiet. The right side of both the bathroom cabinet and
bedroom closet were empty. Michael had always
stored his personal items for the nights he stayed over
on the right because he was left-handed. He claimed
it gave him more elbow room to brush his teeth, blow-
dry his hair and dress.

"Why in the world didn't I object to the way he'd
taken over?" she asked Simba. "It's my house.
Maybe *I* would have preferred the right side."

Somehow she'd allowed herself to get caught up in

Michael's goals, she realized. She'd found herself listening to his advice and convincing herself it was right. When the federal government had asked her to come on board as an animal-disease diagnostician, Michael had convinced her it was an excellent, prestigious career move. So she'd given up a partnership opportunity in a private veterinary clinic in Santa Monica and focused her energies on travel, lab work and lectures.

Simba's tongue snaked out to lick her wrist. His eyes darted away as though he had no idea who'd delivered that sandpapery slobbering caress. It was a vice she'd yet to break him from. Like a chocoholic sneaking sugar, Simba sneaked licks.

Lately, he was the only mammal she cuddled, and that seemed wrong. Her love of animals was part of her life, a soul connection, deep and profound. It was what had compelled her to become a veterinarian in the first place.

The phone rang, and Sunny jumped. She didn't immediately answer, even considered letting the machine pick up. She'd already made four calls, trying to find somebody to hang out with tonight, and every one of them had politely turned her down with some lame excuse.

By damn, she wasn't up to a pity call now—or talking to some shallow gossipmonger spouting false concern just to get the skinny on what had happened between her and Michael.

By the time she got to the phone, the machine had switched on. The sound of her mother's heavy Texas drawl made her stomach lurch.

Just what she needed. A lecture from her mom on the merits of hanging on to a man. Still, nothing said she had to tell her mother about the breakup. Anna Carmichael was clear over in Austin. It wasn't as if she would know what was going on in Los Angeles.

Sighing, Sunny finally reached for the receiver. "I'm here, Mama," she said, cutting off Anna in mid-syllable.

"Oh, I'm so glad I caught you at home. This being a Saturday night, I worried you and Michael would be out."

"Michael's out." *Literally.* "I'm not." *Obviously.*

Anna paused. "Is everything all right? Are you and Michael having troubles?"

Sunny sighed again. Trust her mother to hone in on the "man" angle. Accurately this time, darn it. She ought to keep her mouth shut, but knew she wouldn't. Some strange failing inside her made her feel that she was sinning if she didn't admit every little thing to her mother.

"Michael and I are splitsville."

"Excuse me?"

"We broke up."

"Oh, Sunny. What did you do?"

"Me?" Her voice trembled despite her efforts to keep it even. "Why do you assume it's something *I* did?"

"Perhaps I stated that poorly. You misunderstood."

Sunny didn't think so. She'd spent twenty-nine years trying to measure up to her mother's expectations and Southern standards of what a woman should be. She didn't think she'd hit the mark yet.

"Sunny?" Anna said when the silence stretched. "Are you all right?"

"Yes. I'm fine, Mama."

"Would you like to talk about it?"

''There's not much to say. Michael and I were trying to mesh our calendars and carve out a convenient time for a honeymoon, but he seemed to have a conflict with every date I chose.'' More likely, he hadn't *wanted* to take time off. He'd reminded her that they were both aiming for the top of their respective fields, and it was imperative that they not let the competition get there first.

''He *is* busy, Sunny.''

She felt her insides clench, but continued on with the conversation. ''Yes, but so am I. Which is neither here nor there at the moment, since there won't be a honeymoon, anyway.''

''Is this a problem the two of you might overcome?''

Sunny leaned against the kitchen counter. ''No, Mama. Despite what you might think of me and my single status, I do want children and a family someday. Michael doesn't.''

''Not at all?'' Anna sounded scandalized.

Sunny found she could smile after all. Her mother believed in family, reminded Sunny and her brother, Storm, at every opportunity that she wanted to be a grandmother, that it wasn't fair Trudy Fay Simon continually lorded it over her about her fifth grandchild when Anna had yet to claim even one.

''Not at all,'' Sunny echoed.

''Well. I knew that man wasn't right for you in the first place. He had one of those phony-politician smiles. His teeth were simply too perfect.''

Sunny felt her heart soften. She and her mother had had their trials, but when it came down to it, they were family. And even if they didn't often agree, family stuck together.

"He paid a fortune so those teeth *would* be perfect."

"Figures. So what will you do now?"

"Actually, I've taken some vacation time so I don't have to answer a lot of questions."

"Then I called at the right moment. Come home, Sunny. Your room's just as you left it."

Returning home was an ongoing argument, one they had often. Anna didn't seem to respect or place any importance on what Sunny did in California. "You know I can't—"

"You must. We've got trouble and we need you in Hope Valley. You're the only one we can trust to handle it."

Sunny was momentarily speechless. Her mother had admitted a need. That was a first.

But Sunny could only focus on the words *Hope Valley.* Her hometown was a blip on the Texas map. It lay just west of Austin, where verdant grass carpeted the ground in a feast for the eyes, and livestock grazed contentedly on ranches that ranged from small family operations to million-dollar enterprises. The town was quaint, and truly Southern in attitude. Everyone knew everyone else's business, and the townsfolk accepted it as their God-given right to pass along every morsel of gossip that came their way.

Sunny had been born and raised in Hope Valley. Her family and her childhood friends were there. She'd lived and laughed and loved there.

And she'd had her heart broken there.

What she felt now after her split with Michael was nothing compared to the devastation she'd suffered in Hope Valley ten years earlier.

She twisted the phone cord around her finger and

closed her eyes for a moment to steady herself. Simba, who'd been lying on the cool kitchen floor, scrambled to his feet and pushed against her leg in his canine version of a hug. How this goofy-looking dog was so attuned to her every emotion was uncanny.

"What kind of trouble?"

"On Jack Slade's ranch. Now, hear me out," Anna said, obviously knowing Sunny was about to object. They'd made a shaky deal years ago not to discuss Jackson Slade. Anna didn't always keep up her end of the bargain. Especially when Hope Valley had been close to economic ruin and Jack had returned to town like a prodigal son. He'd taken over his father's ranch and turned it into a highly prosperous spread.

From the moment he'd come back to the small community, everything he touched seemed to thrive. Where once he'd been a motorcycle-riding, earring-wearing, bronc-busting heartbreaker, now he was Hope Valley's golden boy, and there were very few people around these parts who weren't eternally grateful to him. According to Anna Carmichael, the guy had single-handedly made the town flourish once more.

Of course, Anna rarely missed a chance to remind her daughter of what she'd given up.

Sunny rubbed her temples where a headache was forming. "I'm listening."

"This is for your ears only, and it could well be nothing."

"What, Mama?" She wasn't in the mood for a whispering campaign.

"Jack's had some cattle up and die on him. We don't want Hope Valley splashed across the national newspapers, with speculations on mad cow disease or something.''

Her fingers tightened on the receiver. "Does Jack think it's mad cow?" The thought was horrifying. So far, livestock in the United States had escaped that epidemic. More than likely her mother was only using the term because it was familiar.

"I don't know, dear. That's why I'm calling you."

"How many cattle?"

"One or two, I think."

"Only in Jack's herd?"

"So I've heard."

"What does the vet say? What are the symptoms?"

"Honestly, Sunny, I'm not the one to be asking these questions. You need to come see for yourself."

"The vet, Mama…" she prompted.

Anna sighed. "Doc Levin skipped town. We have no earthly idea why. Just packed up his belongings and that young lady he'd taken up with, and left us high and dry. And it's just as well, if you ask me. He never did fit in. We need one of our own here, Sunny. Someone who cares about us. To investigate, to get to the bottom of this sudden illness, give us an unbiased report so we can handle it quickly among ourselves."

That was how the people of Hope Valley had always operated. As a community. "If it's just a couple of steers, that's hardly an epidemic. Still, you know I'm bound by law to report any outbreaks of infectious diseases once they're confirmed."

"Yes, I'm aware of all that, and I'm certainly not advocating we hide anything. But we can trust you not to jump the gun. You're the best there is, Sunny Leigh. The only one who can do this. We don't want to be gettin' the wrong dog by the tail and startin' an uproar of hysteria.''

Sunny slid down the kitchen cabinet and sat on the floor. Her heart pounded and her brain felt fuzzy.

You're the best there is, Sunny Leigh.

How many years had she yearned to hear those words? Words of acceptance. Of praise. From her mother.

This was truly out of character for Anna. Sunny had rarely gotten more than a ''That's nice, dear'' when she'd called home with career news.

Now Jack was in trouble. It bugged her that even after all these years, Anna's immediate concern was for him, not her own daughter. But this was the first time her mother had reached out to her, hinted at pride in Sunny's successes, recognition for the professional she'd become, acceptance of the choices she'd made.

You're the only one who can do this. Powerful words to a woman who'd longed for years to hear them.

Sunny looped her arm around Simba's thick neck. She had a month's vacation and comp time coming to her. Lord knows her life in Los Angeles hadn't turned out the way she'd thought it would.

She could use some weeks away, time to reflect on the influence her relationship with Michael had had on who she'd become.

Because if she was truthful, she'd have to admit that what she'd started out wanting in the beginning had morphed into something entirely different.

She needed to clear her head. Go back to chasing *her* dream. Learn to be a woman who stood firmly on her own two feet, made solid decisions based on the facts as she saw them, and stuck by them.

And by God, the lure of *showing* her mother her expertise was too great to ignore.

Plus, after being abandoned by so-called friends here in California, she found the chance to connect with *true* friends, the kind you could always depend on, was a draw she couldn't resist.

Sunny, Donetta Presley, Tracy Lynn Randolph and Becca Sue Ellsworth had called themselves the Texas Sweethearts. They'd formed their secret society when they were kids. Even years and miles hadn't dampened their bond. Seeing her pals again would be good.

"I'll square things away here and be out there by Wednesday," she said.

The problem was, if an infectious disease *was* plaguing Jackson Slade's cattle, even Wednesday might be too late to save his herd.

THE TEXAS SUN BEAT DOWN on her like flames from hell. A straw Western hat shaded her blond hair, but her T-shirt and jeans felt as though they'd been shrink-wrapped to her body.

Irritated, Sunny imagined ten different scenarios of how she'd kill her mother. She'd been under the impression that Jack's ranch was in crisis. But when she'd arrived at the Forked S ten minutes ago and gone in search of Jack, there didn't appear to be a speck of tension in the air. And none of the hands gave any indication that they recognized her or expected her.

Peachy.

In fact, she'd been told that Jack wasn't even there, although he was due any minute.

"Meddling," she said to the huge dog at her side. "Mama's the Texas state champion at it. I'd lay odds that the minute she discovered Michael was out of the picture, her Southern-lady, all-good-girls-should-be-married-and-settled engine went into overdrive.''

Simba raised his head and gave her a goofy look of agreement, his pink tongue snaking out to bathe her arm with a fast lick.

If matchmaking was Anna's game, Sunny would let her know right quick that she was pulling the wrong sow's ear. Never mind that it was fairly typical behavior. Men always came first with Anna Carmichael. It was in the Southern code. Heck, ten years ago, she'd even advised Sunny to turn a blind eye to Jack's betrayal.

Fat chance. That wasn't Sunny's style. And right now, she'd had it with men. The only male she intended to let close was Simba.

She looped her arm around the dog's neck. Since his wide skull came nearly to her chest, she was able to affectionately hug him for his loyal show of support without bending over.

''See any signs of an airplane yet?''

Simba ignored her question and snapped at a grasshopper that had the misfortune to fly in front of his face.

Instead of watching the private airstrip where Jackson would land, Sunny looked out over the ranch, disregarding the oppressive smell of manure and the stirred-up dust.

The Forked S was some operation, not at all as she'd remembered it from ten years ago. Back then this acreage had been owned by a man who cared more about his next bottle of whiskey than increasing his herd or repairing the outbuildings.

Cattle milled in pens, some bawling as they were squeezed through chutes leading into the corral. Others, dotting the verdant land, munched happily on the feathery grass swaying in the hot summer wind.

Ranch hands in dusty hats, boots and jeans all seemed to have jobs to do and took their duties seriously. No one lazed around smoking in the shade or tipping an icy beer behind the barn.

Evidently, the boss man ran a tight operation.

Sunny took a breath and choked on the cloying, dusty air. Standing in the middle of a ranch that held myriad memories she had no desire to confront was the last thing she'd ever expected to be doing.

She ought to be in Tahiti, floating on a raft in a clear blue bay, drinking sweet, potent concoctions with little umbrellas stuck in a pineapple garnish and licking her emotional wounds in comfort and style.

The drone of a plane engine sent Simba prancing to his feet.

"Yes, I hear it, boy." Sunny shaded her eyes with her hand and watched as a flashy Cessna descended in the blue sky, wings dipping ever so slightly from side to side as the pilot aimed for the short runway. The landing gear seemed about to brush the treetops, and Sunny held her breath. She let it out when the tail cleared the foliage by inches and the Cessna touched down as softly as dandelion fluff. Typical of a hotshot pilot at the controls, Jackson barely slowed the single-engine, blue-and-white plane before putting it into a turn and bringing it around.

"Show-off," she muttered, impressed despite herself. She appreciated skill, admired a person who strove to be the best.

The engine shut off and the two-blade propeller jerked to a stop like a whirligig with a child's finger suddenly thrust into it. After several minutes, the door popped open and Jackson climbed out. He jumped down lithely onto the sticky asphalt, where heat-wave mirages danced over the black surface.

Sunny's heart pumped and sweat trickled down her spine. She was about to come face-to-face with her past.

But she could handle it. She *would* handle it. She'd spent ten long years building a shield around her heart. And a one-month vacation in Texas wasn't going to tear it down.

For a moment he paused, watching her from a distance of one hundred yards. She couldn't see past the aviator sunglasses to his blue eyes, couldn't gauge his mood from his expression because he wore his tobacco-brown Stetson pulled low over his forehead.

Good granny's goose, Jackson Slade still made her mouth water.

Six feet four inches of bad attitude, he drew women like flies to a watermelon, and radiated a masculinity that made a girl want to swoon like a Southern belle of old.

However, Sunny wasn't a Southern belle. Southern, yes, but as much as her mother had tried, her manners were at times abysmal. And swooning wasn't her style.

After the briefest hesitation, he headed toward her, his stride long and loose. If he felt a sense of urgency, it didn't show. Nor did recognition.

That poked at her pride.

Then again, Jackson Slade was a master at hiding his emotions.

He stopped in front of her and stared down at her. As she craned her neck to meet his gaze, the bright sunshine behind him made her eyes water. He shifted subtly so that his body blocked the light. It also crowded her. Deliberately, it seemed.

"Well, if it isn't Miss Sunny Leigh Carmichael."

Damn it, that deep Texas drawl still made her stomach hatch butterflies. She kept her hand on Simba. Not that she was afraid the hound would attack. She didn't think Jack would appreciate Simba's obsession for giving sloppy dog kisses just now.

"Good memory, Slade." She couldn't tell if he was surprised to see her or annoyed.

"You back in town for a visit, sugar bear?"

"Maybe." She wanted him to take off those dark glasses so she could see if he was mocking her. Sugar bear had been his pet name for her all those years ago, at a time when she was certain he'd loved her, certain he'd intended to ask her daddy's permission for her hand in marriage. Well, Daddy was gone now, and Jack had ended up marrying someone else.

"Been a lot of years," he commented, and stepped back. "Any other time I'd be happy to socialize some, but I've got a cow with a possible prolapsed uterus. She's one of my best breeders and if I don't get in there right quick, I'll lose her." His tone implied he was happy for an excuse *not* to be sociable. With her.

Astonished, she stood for several seconds and gaped at his back as he walked away.

Who the heck had put a burr up his behind? The man had cheated on her ten years ago and had had a child with another woman, while Sunny had nursed a bone-deep hurt and pined—yes, darn it, *pined*—for him.

If *anyone* should be acting bitchy here, it should be her!

Miffed by his attitude, she considered leaving. But her conscience as a veterinarian forced her to stay.

If Jack's dead cattle turned out to be nothing more than routine, she was off the hook. In the meantime, she'd made a promise to her mother to look into the matter. And when Sunny made a promise, she didn't break it.

Unlike Jackson Slade.

Chapter Two

Sunny jogged to catch up with him. "Mind if I tag along?"

"Can I stop you?"

"Doubt it."

"Then stay out of my way, and keep that mangy-looking horse outside. What the hell is it, anyway?"

Again, Sunny was taken aback by Jack's brusqueness. It didn't make sense. Unless he *did* know why she was here and he had something to hide. Some ranchers abhorred government intrusion or help. She'd stared down the barrel of more than one shotgun during her career.

"*It* is a he, and his name is Simba. Lab and Irish wolfhound mix."

Jack snorted and continued through the double doors of a steel outbuilding that bore a sign proclaiming it the Forked S Calving Shed.

The urge to stick out her tongue at his back was strong, but she resisted. Instead, she dropped a kiss on Simba's huge head and told him to wait for her by the door.

Sure, Simba was odd-looking—she'd often wondered if he'd come from the same litter as the comic-strip character Marmaduke. Regardless, that was no reason to insult him.

If there was one thing that could make her forget her problems, it was squaring off with Jack Slade.

She removed her hat, leaving Simba in charge of it, then ran her fingers through her blond hair in an attempt to get rid of the ''hat hair'' look.

''I think I'm going to enjoy taking this macho cowboy down a notch or two,'' she muttered, and followed Jack inside.

The calving shed was well lit and scrubbed clean, Sunny noted, with gleaming white walls, concrete floors and plenty of drains. Three ranch hands were bending over a very large, extremely irritated black Angus who lay on her side on the floor, held steady in a head catch, legs tied, eyes rolling in pain and anger. Although the working area appeared properly sterilized, the familiar smells of hay, leather and bovine fluids permeated the air.

''What's the deal, Scotty?'' she heard Jack ask as he whipped off his sunglasses and hat and stepped into a pair of dingy blue coveralls. Despite their faded color, the creases clearly indicated they were clean.

''I tried to pull the calf, but it was too durn big. Dadgumit, why'd Doc Levin up and quit on us?''

Sunny had wondered that, too—her mother hadn't known—but Jack just shrugged. ''We'll have to handle this ourselves.''

This meaning a C-section, Sunny understood.

''Is Keegan back yet?''

''Nope,'' Scotty said. ''Not yet.''

Jack uttered a curse. ''I should have had Beau go for supplies and kept Duane here.''

''Mighta' had a bit of a scuffle over that,'' Scotty

said, absently patting the distressed cow. "Beau's up to the house, fussin' with Miz Cora over the kitchen. He's cookin' up a fancy soufflé and claims her vacuumin's gonna make it fall or some such nonsense. Nearly took my head off when I poked my nose in for a cool drink." Scotty shook his head. "You find something when you were up in the air?"

On alert, Sunny waited for his answer. Evidently, Duane Keegan was Jack's right-hand man and he was needed back on the ranch ASAP.

"Maybe," Jack mumbled noncommittally. "Right now we've got to see to this mama or we'll lose both cow and calf."

Sunny's shoulders slumped. Obviously, he didn't cotton to speaking in front of outsiders—her. Another indication that her being at the ranch was her mother's doing, that Jack hadn't asked her to come.

He stepped up to the sink, began washing his hands and arms. "Scotty, get the clippers and check her spinal. Lou, grab the instruments and a new scalpel. Junior, you got the lidocaine ready?"

"Got it, boss."

Jackson glanced at Sunny as though just remembering she was there. His eyes were even bluer than she recalled, and his deep walnut hair now showed signs of gray at the temples.

"This could get a bit gory for you, sugar. Might want to close those pretty green eyes."

Oh, gag me.

"If I close my eyes, *sugar,* how can I critique your procedure?"

His brow lifted. "You intend to criticize?"

"Maybe."

"So you haven't learned to curb that sassy tongue

any, hmm? Do you still say whatever comes to mind?''

''Oh, I imagine I've managed a little restraint over the years.''

''Except when it comes to criticizing—to hanging a person without a trial.''

He gazed at her, and she knew he was recalling a time ten years ago when she *hadn't* spoken her mind, hadn't waited around for explanations.

She wasn't going to be dragged into that discussion. He'd moved on with his life and so had she. No reason for explanations when her eyes had *seen* all she'd needed to.

''If you don't step it up a bit, Slade,'' she said, ''no judge or jury in the world's gonna save this mama from a death sentence.''

A muscle tightened in his jaw. ''If you insist on staying, you might as well scrub up. I don't want you wandering around and contaminating my operating room. This here's a bit different from watching little mice run around on treadmills.''

''Is that what you think I do?''

''Frankly, sugar bear, I don't really know what you do. Heard tell you were some fancy scientist, though.''

She was annoyed that he'd dismissed her profession so quickly—and inaccurately. He didn't believe she knew squat about what he was fixing to do, and obviously figured he would gross her out cutting into the belly of a cow.

Besides making a snap judgment about her abilities, did he believe she'd turned into a sissy? Well, by dog, over the next few weeks he was going to find out exactly how qualified she was.

But this whole situation could well end up beyond

her control. If there was a potential epidemic, people higher up in the food chain than her would step in and take over. She hoped like crazy things wouldn't come to that point.

This was her hometown, too. Hope Valley had nearly folded awhile back. Jack's return had provided jobs. He'd invested in the town, infused life back into it. Despite what was between them personally, she had to admire him for that.

But if he went down, it would affect her friends and family, as well.

She was going to make sure that didn't happen—or at least, try to lessen the impact of it.

Since Jack hadn't bothered to introduce her to his men, they kept giving her sidelong glances even as they went about their business of saving the life of the heifer and calf.

Electric clippers buzzed as Scotty shaved a three-foot section on the cow's side. Jack lifted the tail and let it drop, checking for resistance to gauge the progress of the spinal. He was clearly impatient, worried, yet was making sure the animal wouldn't feel pain.

Sunny had known others who weren't so compassionate.

"Okay, give me the lidocaine, Junior." With the needle, Jack scratched a thin line down the middle of the shaved area, then injected the topical anesthetic every inch or so along it in case there were any areas not numbed by the spinal. He quickly followed the route with a scalpel, cutting in one long stroke through the tough hide. A ribbon of blood blossomed in the scalpel's wake, and he squirted more lidocaine into the incision before he cut deeper.

When the wound gaped, a gush of blood from the cut splattered them.

"Damn it! I've got bleeders. I need a clamp. Somebody get in here and—"

Sunny deftly plucked a clamp off the metal tray and slapped it in his palm.

"Thanks," he mumbled, his breathing returning to normal when the spurt slowed to a trickle. He put his hands inside the incision and gently held up the uterus so that it partly protruded from the cow's abdomen. "Lou, I need some help here. Take the scalpel and—"

"Wait," Sunny interrupted. "His shirt has long sleeves."

Jack glanced at her, clearly impatient. "And your point?"

"My point is if he goes into this cow in long sleeves, he'll kill her. The bacteria on that material might as well be a shot of pure poison." She took up the scalpel herself.

"Yeah, and if you slip and perforate her uterus she's dead, too. That outer layer's like tissue paper."

"Then why don't you shut up and hold still? You're not the only one around here who grew up on a cattle ranch. There." Ignoring his scowl, she opened the sac of glistening white muscle, and laughed gaily when a pair of hooves popped free.

"Oh, aren't you a beauty! Take it quickly, Scotty," she said, and scooted back as the older man swung the solid black calf from its mamma's belly. Shifting on her knees, she cleaned out its mouth as Scotty cradled it.

"Is that calf okay?" Jack asked over his shoulder as he tended to the heifer.

"Seems to be," Scotty said.

Sunny glanced up, knew she was grinning like a loon but couldn't help it. The birth of any living thing was such a miracle. It had been too long since she'd experienced it. Normally, by the time she was called out to a ranch, it was to deal with death and disease.

"I need those pills," Jack barked, though his gaze lingered on her for a moment, his blue eyes softening with respect.

Although she didn't think he was speaking to her, Sunny located the large pink antibiotics on the steel tray and dropped them into the cow's uterus. Jack glanced at her again, his expression unreadable.

"Appears you've got some experience with this sort of thing," he commented as he began to stitch up the incision.

"I watched Daddy and old Doc Porter perform a few C-sections when I was a kid." That he hadn't known this struck her as odd. "The rest of the experience came from six years of intensive study at the University of California at Davis School of Veterinary Medicine."

"You're a vet?" His tone was tinged with surprise, curiosity and something else she couldn't identify. "I thought you worked in a science lab studying animals."

"Guess you were misinformed." Had he asked about her? The thought made her feel fluttery.

"California," he murmured, then looked directly at her. "The land of sunshine and sin hasn't chased away that Texas drawl any."

"I decided that keeping it was to my advantage. It's amazing what a Southern whisper does to a man," she taunted.

His gaze dropped to her mouth. "I'll say one thing

for you, sugar bear. You're the only woman I've met whose voice could make a guy imagine he's smelling magnolias and tasting fine whiskey at the same time.''

''Compliments, Slade?''

He shrugged. ''I've been known to give them a time or two.''

''And I'm a woman who likes them. How about you?'' she asked. ''Where'd you learn to doctor cattle?''

''Same as you…'' His gaze lifted slowly. ''Without the fancy education, that is. I watched and one day I had to just jump in and do it. Trial by fire.'' A cocky smile tipped the corners of his lips. ''Guess you already know that, with you being a vet and all. Though I imagine this here mama's a bit more cumbersome to work with than your usual poodles and wiener dogs.''

She chuckled. If he only knew. ''A bit.''

''Do you have a practice?''

''A private one, no.'' She discreetly inspected the cow for signs of disease, aware that an asymptomatic animal like this one would probably require blood tests and lab equipment. Outward signs of disease or not, every head of cattle on this ranch would have to be examined and tested to see if there was indeed an outbreak of infection, as her mother had led her to believe.

So far, Jack hadn't said a word about any problems, and oddly enough, she wanted him to seek her advice on his own. With her government credentials, she didn't need an invitation to show up on someone's property, but waiting until asked was courteous.

Besides, she wasn't here officially—yet.

An incredible feeling of satisfaction swept over her as she ministered to the newborn, stroked her hand over its wet, sticky coat. A perfectly healthy little bull. She gazed back at the mama cow, imagining that she saw gratitude in those big, beautiful brown eyes. Sunny had helped save two lives today. Her sense of accomplishment made her euphoric.

Sudden memories whirled in her mind, evoked by the familiar smells of the barn, and the neigh of horses nearby; memories of the foal she'd delivered at age fourteen and the coyote she'd bottle-fed and stayed up nights with after its mother had strayed too close to a steel trap. She glanced down at the scar on her hand, a permanent reminder from an injured owl that had ripped away flesh when she'd tried to bandage its wing.

What had happened to that young girl? she wondered. She'd spent the past few years determined to prove herself, to climb the ladder of success, yet every rung had seemingly taken her further away from who she really was, what she'd started out wanting.

To be the best veterinarian around.

She'd traded her blue jeans for business suits and lab coats. Thinking about it now, she couldn't remember the last time she'd truly felt in her element—as she did here, helping to save the life of a cow and her calf.

She watched as Jack worked a needle and silk through the cow's exposed layers, mesmerized by the capability of his hands—hands that had caressed her body a very long time ago; hands that had made silent promises. Those promises had never been kept.

"You could probably stitch up this heifer better than I can," he said.

She blinked and ordered her mind to stay on task.

''No 'probably' about it, Slade. I'd have had it done by now.''

He surprised her with a burst of laughter. ''Still competitive, I see.''

She looked across at him, snagged his gaze, made sure she had his attention. ''Yes. And I still don't like to share.''

He didn't even wince, the jerk. ''I'll keep that in mind.''

Sunny felt like a fool for giving even that much of herself away. She didn't want Jack to know that she still remembered what they'd once had together, what he'd thrown away. And she shouldn't be thinking about that in the first place. For crying out loud, only a week ago she'd been engaged to another man.

''You're not gonna get sick on me, are you, Carmichael?''

She glanced up, deliberately tucked away her emotions. ''That's *Dr.* Carmichael, if you don't mind. And fat chance of me getting sick during a C-section.''

He shrugged. ''Looked a little green around the gills for a minute. My mistake.''

Despite the cavalier way he'd delivered his words, she could have sworn she'd seen a spark of concern in his eyes. And *that* was ridiculous, she told herself, focusing on the heifer, who looked as wrung out as every new mother had a right to.

He sutured the thin layer of the peritoneum, taking some muscle tissue with it, then moved on to the actual muscle and fascia. ''How's that calf, Scotty?'' he asked. ''Bull or heifer?''

''Bull,'' Scotty relayed. ''He's doing fine.''

''Then go ahead and tag him, give him a shot and put him in the jug.''

"Alone?" Scotty asked, glancing toward the stalls where they usually put mothers and babies together.

Jack's hands stilled for a moment. "Yes. Alone."

Quarantine. At least he had sense enough—integrity enough—to do that. Sunny had noted that most of his cattle didn't bear ear marks. Breeders of high-grade stock didn't always use them, feeling the knife cuts detracted from the head at a sale.

Was he tagging this one as a means of keeping track of a developing disease? She waited to see if he'd confide in her, ask her opinion as a professional veterinarian, admit what he was facing.

His chiseled features remained expressionless.

When he stood and moved to the washbasin, she followed him. She could feel the warmth of his big body as their shoulders nearly touched.

Scooting a bit to the side, she let the tepid water run over her hands as he used the soap. Rust-colored remains from the birth swirled over the bottom of the scarred porcelain sink as iridescent bubbles burst like fragile dreams.

If he wasn't going to divulge the problem, she'd have to prod. "You told Scotty to isolate the calf. Are you quarantining, then?"

JACK FELT HIS HEART SKIP. The soap slipped from his fingers as he whipped his head around. His gaze collided with Sunny's steady look. "Why would you ask that?"

She sighed. "My mother called."

"And?"

"And I'm not simply an accredited vet, Jack. I work for the government, specializing in infectious diseases in large animals."

"Nobody said anything about infectious disease."

"You don't have a couple of dead cows?"

"One. Only one dead cow. Nothing to suggest we have an epidemic or that the death was from a contagious disease. If I thought I had a problem, I'd have called the Department of Agriculture."

"Guess I saved you a quarter, then."

"I just said I didn't have a problem." He didn't need a bunch of bureaucrats crawling around, telling him how to do his business.

He went still when she put a wet hand on his wrist. Ten long years had passed since he'd felt her touch. Ten years of trying to get the memory out of his mind.

He shifted and her hand fell away.

"Jack, I'm not here as a government employee. I'm on vacation. You might as well take advantage of my expertise."

"Why?"

"Because Doc Levin's gone. Hope Valley is without a vet, and I'm licensed to work in the state of Texas. You need help and I'm available."

"I don't need some hotshot lady on a power trip overreacting and shutting me down—"

"Hold it. You're not in a good position to insult me or tick me off. This happens to be my town, too, and I've got a stake in it."

She was working up a head of steam. Awed, he kept his mouth shut and watched her.

"I'm not here for you," she continued. "I'm here for Hope Valley, for Vince over at the meat market, for Donetta and her customers at the beauty shop, for Tracy Lynn and her endless causes, for…" She waved as though reaching for another name in the air.

Jack stepped back in case she decided to clobber

him. Her tanned cheeks had taken on a rosy hue, and a sexy vein he'd like to spend awhile studying pulsed at her temple. She was at least a foot shorter than him, but a man would be wise not to underestimate her.

"I'm doing this for my brother—"

"Your brother?" Jack had to interrupt before she lost him completely. "He's the sheriff."

"Yes. And if the ranchers around here go belly-up, the place will turn into a ghost town. There won't be anyone to keep the peace for. No drunks to toss in jail or parking tickets to issue for the town's revenue. No one in need of legal counsel."

He felt a smile tug at his lips. "Bloodthirsty, aren't we?"

She glared, her green eyes glinting like polished jade caught by the sun.

"I get the point, sugar."

She snatched at a paper towel and unrolled half the roll. He helpfully held the cylinder steady for her.

"Thank you."

"You're welcome." He dried his hands and tossed the used paper in the trash.

"How long ago did your cow die?" she asked.

"Last week."

"Did you note any symptoms, have anyone do an examination?"

He shook his head. He was still upset over that, but mistakes happened. "My foreman found her. He was out riding the range, checking a downed fence. The cow was already dead. Duane said there were lesions, evidence of foamy saliva. By the time I got out there, he'd burned the carcass."

"Damn."

"Yeah. My sentiments exactly." Though he'd expressed them a little more strongly, he recalled. He couldn't really fault his foreman. Duane had been on the rodeo circuit for most of his life. He hadn't yet learned all there was to know about ranching. "Duane panicked."

She sighed. "He wouldn't be the first. You never answered me. Have you established a control zone as a precaution?"

"Yes. A six-mile square for that herd. Like I said, the incident appears isolated." He saw her checking out his calving shed, knew she couldn't find fault with the clean walls and concrete floors, or with Scotty, Lou and Junior's diligent sterilizing procedures. Though she had made a damn good call about Lou's long-sleeved shirt.

She wore her blond hair shorter now, he noted, but obviously had never tamed all those glorious curls she'd lamented at one time. Her skin was clear and smooth; her mouth bore the remnants of a subtle pink gloss. Even in blue jeans and a sleeveless red shirt, she still looked classy. Not at all like a veterinarian. Or a government official.

"Jack?"

"What?" He realized she'd been speaking. And he'd been zoned out, way too close to taking a trip down memory lane. A trip he had no intention of embarking on. They'd tried to make a go of it once. The relationship had bombed and he wasn't going to stick his hand in for another detonation.

"I said I'd still like to have a look around."

"Show off your credentials?" The corner of her eye twitched. He recognized the movement. Although her shoulders squared, he'd hit a nerve. "Hell, that was nasty. I'm just edgy. I'm sorry."

Her pale brows lifted. "An apology?"

"Don't get too used to it."

She grinned and an unwelcome wave of desire slammed into his gut. Her mama had named her aptly. Because when Sunny smiled, she could brighten even the gloomiest day.

"If you want to check out the health of my livestock, I won't stop you."

"Spoken like a true Southern gentleman."

The little minx could still deliver subtle sarcasm with a dollop of syrup. That he was on the verge of falling all over himself annoyed him.

"Since I'm on a roll, I suppose I could offer my surgical assistant a glass of tea before she leaves." After shrugging out of his coveralls, he led the way out of the calving shed and into the bright sunlight. Her sudden arrival after all these years had caught him off guard.

"And I'll take you up on the offer. I could use something cold before I get to work."

He shook his head. "It's late in the day, Sunny. It's not as if we're in an immediate crisis. It'll keep."

"Tomorrow, then."

"I don't have time to play tour guide tomorrow."

"Are you avoiding me?"

"No. I have a ranch to run. Folks usually call ahead when they want a chunk of my time."

"I came under the impression I was invited."

"Not by me."

"I realize that now. My mother and I are going to have a talk."

"Don't be too hard on her. She means well."

"What is it with you and my mother? You both jump to support the other's side."

"Your mother thinks I'm charming," he said with an easy shrug.

Sunny snorted, but Jack didn't take offense. He couldn't say why, but he had a soft spot in his heart for Anna Carmichael. Maybe because she'd always given him the benefit of the doubt, made him feel that he could be something. He knew Sunny and her mother hadn't always gotten along, and that puzzled him. After his own mother had died, he would have given anything to be part of a family like the Carmichaels.

Still, he wished Anna had consulted him before calling Sunny. He didn't even question how she'd found out about his worry. Anna and his housekeeper, Cora, gabbed on the phone incessantly.

But he and Sunny were getting off track, he realized. She was still hell-bent on examining his herd. Granted, he'd welcome the advice of a veterinarian, but the fact that the vet in question happened to be Sunny Carmichael bugged him. He needed a chance to figure out why.

"When did you get into town?" he asked.

"This morning."

"Then take tomorrow and settle in. Friday's soon enough to poke around out here. Besides, I'd like a chance to prepare the men. I don't want any unnecessary alarms or false rumors spreading."

"Fine," she said. "I guess I'll have to trust your judgment for the moment about the urgency of this case."

"It's *not* a case, damn it."

SUNNY DECIDED TO BACK OFF and change the subject. Jack was clearly touchy.

She couldn't make him cooperate at this stage. It was his property.

Until another episode occurred or he asked for her help, she was simply a veterinarian on vacation who was making a neighborly courtesy call at the behest of her mother.

And a woman who had too many unresolved memories of Jackson Slade.

Chapter Three

As they headed toward the main house, Sunny plucked her straw hat out of Simba's mouth and tried to ignore the teeth marks in the brim.

"The skies were clear when you landed awhile back, but this humidity feels higher than an owl's IQ."

"You've been gone too long, sugar bear. You've gotten soft."

"I'll say one thing for California, the weather's paradise." *Great. Reduced to talking about the weather. Scintillating conversation, Sunny.* "And if you don't mind, I'd just as soon you quit with the sugar bear stuff."

One dark eyebrow cocked beneath the brim of the Stetson shading his face. "Seems I recollect a time when you'd nearly melt if I called you sugar bear. Remember, Sun?" he asked softly. They'd stopped close to the back door of the house, his tone nearly paralyzing her. It was a gift, the way he could render a woman mute with a mere change in tone, a deepening of his voice, an intimate rasp. "You'd go all dreamy, put those smooth hands all over my body, climb right up me..." His voice was barely audible now, still raspy, and with a definite bite. *"Sugar bear."*

This time the endearment was a taunt.

Her body quaked. Arousal had come swift and hard. Even now it continued to hold her in its grip. But damn his blue eyes, she would *not* reveal it. She wasn't a gullible eighteen-year-old who believed in happily ever after. Oh, her parents had had thirty-five years of lasting true love before Daddy had died, but they'd been another generation; they'd been the exception to the rule.

"Vivid memory, Slade. From that description, most people would assume you'd had a pretty damn good thing going. Too bad you couldn't keep your pants zipped when Lanette McGreavy came flashing her boobs and bubble butt in your face." Annoyed that he'd pushed her into bringing up the past, which was the *last* thing she'd wanted to do, Sunny said, "I think I'll take a rain check on that tea. I'm feeling about as civil as a preacher with the devil camped out in his backyard."

Jackson's lips twitched. Twitched! Either the man didn't have enough sense to spit downwind, or he had a death wish. You simply didn't *twitch* in the presence of a majorly annoyed female.

"Brother Glen laughs in the face of the devil, sugar bea— Sugar," he corrected, eyes twinkling.

"Sunny," she countered, though his calling her "sugar" was all right. It was an expression everyone used in the South. Grandma Birdie called her "sugar." Her best friends called her "sugar." As long as he didn't tack on the "bear" part, she'd let it slide.

And why, she asked herself, did it take only a sexy twinkle in his blue eyes and a quirk of his lips to mollify her, make her regret her quick tongue? Couldn't the exasperating man pick a mood and stick with it?

Now what was she supposed to do? Should she stay for tea and let him know he could reduce her to mush with a crook of his finger, or should she spite herself and run like a scared rabbit?

For the first time, he actually reached out and touched her. He must have thought she was preparing to leave, because his hand cupped her shoulder, eased down her arm, hesitated over her hand for a moment, then let go.

"Come in out of the heat, Sunny. I'd like you to meet my daughter."

Flight or fight warred once again. She knew he had a daughter—Donetta had told her that much before Sunny had cut her off, saying she didn't want to hear anything about Jackson Slade and his family. She'd made Donetta swear on her grandmother's eyes that if he should ask about her she wouldn't give him even a kernel of information.

Sunny Ostrich Carmichael. Sticking her head in the sand, rather than facing that Jack had slept with another woman, married her, had a child with her.

Donetta had kept her part of the bargain, and never mentioned Jack or his life. Anna Carmichael had not been bound by such a promise, though, and just that morning had imparted the juicy tidbit to Sunny that there was no longer a *Mrs.* Slade in residence.

Still, at the mention of a daughter Sunny couldn't help uttering a snide dig. "What about your wife? Will she be showing up for tea, as well? To pick up her daughter, perhaps?"

"Be a little tough to accomplish, since she's dead."

"Oh, God, Jack. I'm sorry." She felt like a heel. Why had her mother bothered to remark on the absence of his wife, yet not tell her the full details? Never mind that Sunny tended to cut her off every time Anna talked about Jack. For once she wished her mother hadn't paid attention to her admonitions.

He shrugged. "I'm not a grieving widower. Lanette divorced me three years ago."

"Oh." Still, Sunny felt awful. To speak ill of a rival was one thing; to pick on the deceased was quite another. That was uncalled for, and even Sunny had better manners than that. Now she felt bad for making the remark about Lanette's bubble butt—never mind that it was the truth… *Oh, for pity's sake, Sunny! Now, quit!*

"Tea would be very nice, thank you," she said like a perfect Southern lady, as though the invitation had just been extended and the other stuff hadn't gotten in the way.

She gave Simba a pat and a hug. "Sorry, boy. People just don't understand what a pussycat you are. So wait for me outside, okay? And *please* try not to lick anyone."

Simba's ears lowered and he looked away.

"Oh, stop it," she said. "You know I hate it when you guilt-trip me."

"Uh, Sunny?"

She looked up at Jack.

"Do you honestly think that…canine, for lack of a better word, understands you?"

"Of course he does. You'll see. He'll wait patiently by the door. He might even get ambitious and sweep the porch."

Jack shook his head as though he feared for her

sanity, then opened the back door and waited like a gentleman for her to precede him. She caught him staring at her backside, and though her nerves scrambled, she felt a sense of feminine power.

Eat your heart out, pal.

The delicious smell of rich chocolate and yeast permeated the kitchen of Jack's ranch house, creating instant nostalgia. A long time had gone by since she'd been surrounded by the scents of homebaking. Despite the obvious heat from the oven, the air conditioner was doing its duty and more; the chill air actually made her shiver after the sticky heat of outdoors.

An old man, tall and skinny, with the bow-legged stance of a guy who'd spent the better part of his life on a horse stood in front of the oven, wearing thick, red gingham mitts, a white chef's apron and a scowl. He belligerently faced off with a plump, rosy-cheeked woman who also wore a bib apron—this one adorned with a tiny rosebud pattern that Sunny recognized. She had an apron exactly like it stuffed in a drawer in California, along with a bunch of other kitchen items her mother had helpfully sent and Sunny had never used.

The man was Beau Thompson, the number-one cowboy on the ranch despite his age. He'd earned the position thirty times over, as he'd been here before Jack had been born. The woman, of course, was Cora Harriet, Jack's housekeeper and possessor of the violent vacuum, who'd be held responsible if the soufflé flopped.

A little girl with blond hair hanging to her waist looked up when they entered. Immediately, she scooted out of her chair and ran to Jack. He hoisted her up and gave her a smacking kiss on the cheek. Her thin, tanned arms wrapped around his neck and clung for a long moment, then loosened reluctantly as he set her down.

"Victoria, I'd like you to meet a friend of mine. This is Sunny Carmichael. Sunny, my daughter, Tori."

"Hey, cutie pie," Sunny said. The girl had huge brown eyes, beautifully smooth skin kissed by the sun and lips most supermodels dreamed about and rarely received except by collagen injections. She was small for her age, appearing closer to six than nine.

Tori Slade didn't look a thing like her father. Which meant she must resemble her mother. Hard to tell, since Lanette McGreavy had painted her face like a cheap streetwalker on Sunset Boulevard, the makeup so thick no one really knew what she looked like beneath it.

Oh, the devil take it all, there she went again. Pickin' on a dead woman. She was ashamed of herself.

"Hey," Tori whispered back. "It's very nice to meet you, Miz Carmichael." After uttering the shy, excruciatingly polite words, she clung to her father's side and laid her cheek against his hip as though she expected someone to snatch her away. Her doe eyes were solemn, too solemn for a nine-year-old.

Despite the circumstances of Tori's birth, Sunny was drawn to the young girl.

"Call me Sunny, okay?" Squatting on one knee, which put her at eye level with Jack's crotch—it simply couldn't be helped, given the way Tori clung to his side—Sunny meant to gentle the girl, to telegraph that she wasn't an enemy, that she might even be an ally.

That was when she realized the half-inch-thick

necklace draped around Tori's shoulders and chest was moving.

A snake.

A harmless garter snake, yes, but still a snake.

Sunny was a top-notch veterinarian. The very best in her field. But she *hated* snakes.

Instinctively, before she could check her reaction, she gave a typically feminine, one-note squeak and jerked back, to land right on her butt, embarrassing the hell out of herself as she craw-fished away as fast and far as she could go.

Obviously responding to his mistress's distress, Simba slammed his huge body against the slightly open door and charged into the kitchen, slipping on the tiles, knocking over chairs as though they were bowling pins and he a heavy ball.

Beau started hollering loud enough to disturb the skeletons at Darwin's Cemetery. Cora hugged the wall, crossing herself the way Catholics did in fright, repentance or gratitude, even though Sunny knew the woman was Southern Baptist.

"What in tarnation is *that?*" Beau shouted, pointing to Simba, then whirling around to look through the oven's glass at his delicate concoction.

"Dadgumit, it's ruined. Ruined, I tell you! First that fool woman comes in here sucking a perfectly clean floor with the Hoover, vibrating the floorboards and settin' my cake pans to rattling—" he pointed a finger accusingly at Cora "—then *you* start screeching like a mashed cat." He glowered at Sunny.

Turning his ire on Simba, who'd recovered his balance and was panting happily, eyeing Tori's head as an excellent target to lick, Beau threw up his mitten-covered hands. "Then the ugliest miniature horse I've

ever laid eyes on comes slidin' into my kitchen all
spraddle-legged, the likes of something I ain't ever
seen 'cept on them cartoons Tori's so fond of. Now,
does somebody want to tell me how my perfectly fine
morning went to hell so quick?''

''Watch your language, you old goat,'' Cora admonished, the only soul in the room brave enough to
speak just now.

Beau harrumped. ''Beg pardon, Miss Victoria.'' He
opened the oven and took out his egg confection,
which was sadly inverted rather than a puffy, airy
dome.

Cora rolled her eyes. ''There are other women in
the room besides Miss Tori.''

''Woman,'' Beau snapped. ''I begged pardon, and
it ought to suffice for everyone in the whole damned
house—beg pardon again, Miss Tori—and you know
good and well you was admonishing my bad manners
in front of the young 'un, not the other two of you.''

Sunny had recovered her wits and, giving Tori and
her snake a wide berth, moved next to Simba. She
looped her arm around his neck lest he be insulted or
give in to the urge she could see in his eyes to bestow
a couple of doggie kisses on Tori. She had no idea
how her pet would react if he performed one of his
walk-by lickings and got a tongueful of snake. He'd
likely destroy the furniture—heck, *she'd* likely destroy
the furniture if that snake touched her.

''All right,'' Jack said, obviously thinking that
someone ought to regain control and, being the one
who paid the bills, he was elected. ''I believe that just
about covers all the beg pardons and finger-pointing.''
He gazed at Sunny. ''I see you haven't gotten over

your fear of snakes. Seems that'd be a handicap for a vet.''

''I've managed to work around it,'' she said, ignoring his surprise and curiosity. ''And we're not quite finished begging pardons. At least, I'm not. Beau, I apologize for Simba running into your kitchen this way and messing up your soufflé. He's a marshmallow, but he's protective of me in his own silly way. If someone was actually trying to hurt me, about the extent of his aggression would be to sit on the person and lick him to death. He's really a good dog. He's just huge.''

Beau studied her for a minute, and the twinkle in his eye told her he was a big bluffer.

''Apology accepted, Miss Sunny. And welcome home. You've been missed.'' His pale blue eyes moved from her to Jack and back again.

Oh, no, she wanted to say. *Don't even act as though you're remembering that!*

Years ago, Beau had caught Sunny and Jack in the hayloft, half-dressed. He'd merely said, ''Boy, I hope to hell you got rubbers in your pocket. If you don't, then you'd best restore that young lady's clothes and go douse yourself in the horse trough.''

From the time their relationship had turned intimate, Jack had never been without condoms in his pocket. But after getting caught by Beau that time, neither one of them could concentrate, which had put an end to their evening—more than likely just as Beau had intended.

Even after all these years, Sunny felt her face flame at the memory, and she had a great deal of trouble meeting Beau's eyes—or Jack's, for that matter.

Only a week later, her relationship with Jack had gone to hell.

One extra stoplight while driving through town might have changed the course of her life. But every signal had been green, every cosmic force on earth aligned perfectly…perfectly enough to shatter her heart.

Looking at him now, noting the sex appeal oozing out of his pores like sweet temptation, Sunny knew she wasn't immune to him. Ten years could have been ten minutes.

And during her stay in Hope Valley, she'd have a difficult time hanging tough against that much maleness.

But she would. She had to investigate the possible outbreak of a contagious livestock disease in her hometown. If it proved out, it would tag Hope Valley with a nasty stigma forevermore, destroy the local economy and be written about in research journals and history books.

Mostly, though, she would hang tough because she would *not* allow anyone to break her heart ever again.

Especially Jackson Slade, the testosterone-laden cowboy who was eyeing her from across the kitchen with a masculine confidence that silently stated he had no doubt he could get lucky again anytime he wanted.

If the room hadn't been full of people with listening ears, she'd have told him right quick that he'd be picking cockleburs out of a skunk's rear end before that happened.

Chapter Four

Sunny was hot and tired, and her nerves were screaming because she'd been in proximity with Jack again, but when she left his ranch, she picked up her cell phone and dialed Donetta's number.

Her friend answered on the third ring. "Donetta's Secret."

"Hey, girlfriend. You busy?"

There was a pause. "Sunny? Where are you? You said you were coming home, and I've been expecting you all day."

"I had to make a business stop first."

"Jack's ranch?"

"Does *everybody* know *everything?*"

"Silly question. Of course we do."

Sunny grinned. "It's good to hear your voice, Donetta."

"Ditto. But I'd much rather see your ugly mug than just talk to you."

"You're such a pal. Can Simba come to the shop if he promises to behave?"

Donetta laughed. "Simba's always welcome. We'll perm his hair."

"Don't you dare suggest that in front of him." She could picture Donetta rolling her eyes, and smiled.

"Tracy Lynn and Becca Sue are already here. We're waiting for you."

"I'll be there in ten minutes."

She turned off the phone and stepped on the gas, lowering the power window on her Suburban to let the warm Texas breeze tangle in her hair. Simba crowded forward in the back seat and hung his head out the window, his ears flapping in the wind.

The smell of freshly mowed alfalfa wafted in. There weren't many cars on the two-lane road, and fields lined both sides of the highway, creating a restful, familiar sight. In California, she'd gotten used to bumper-to-bumper freeway traffic, and buildings and houses crammed into every available space. To look out and see the horizon was nice.

As she drove into Hope Valley, echoes from the past engulfed her. The town itself encompassed about six square blocks, with the school, hospital and library on the outskirts. On the main drag was the drugstore, where Donetta had dared Sunny to buy a package of condoms, and Mr. Chandler had promptly called Grandma Birdie to report the incident; Grandma Birdie had been known to step out on occasion with the widower Chandler.

Sunny passed Hope Motel—to which she and Jack had sneaked off after her senior prom—the grocery store, hardware store and saddle shop. She slowed in front of Wanda's Diner. She and her friends had hung out drinking sodas and ruining their supper on Wanda's famous French Fries—until good old Lanette McGreavy had set her sights on Jack and sent Sunny's world spiraling.

She wasn't going to think about that.

Two doors down from Donetta's hair salon was Becca's Attic. Becca had always been the Texas Sweetheart who imagined herself a lady in the 1800s. *Ha,* Sunny thought. Becca's love of history and frilly things might have served her well in the olden days, but society wouldn't have been ready for her outspoken ways.

After pulling the SUV into a parking spot in front of Donetta's Secret, Sunny got out, and had to grab the door for support when Simba nearly knocked her down in his exuberant leap from the back seat.

"Mind your manners, or I'll let Donetta put curlers in your hair." Simba's ears lowered and he hugged her side. "I'm just kidding. I wouldn't let her mess with your masculinity that way. But you do have to be good."

By rote, she secured her vehicle, the alarm chirping as she pushed the button on her remote control. Probably half the pickup trucks lining the curb had their keys in the ignition. That was the way Hope Valley was. Everyone watched out for everyone else and everyone else's property. It was a good town with good people.

After the sticky heat outdoors, the air-conditioned salon felt heavenly.

Sunny paused at the doorway, and everything within her shifted. Simba was hidden from view by the reception desk, and due to the noise and activity, no one had noticed their arrival. Gratefully, she took a moment to steady her rushing emotions.

Home.

She hadn't realized how much she'd missed it until just now.

The smell of bleach and perm solution filled the air. Country music coming out of a portable boom box vied with the hum of hair dryers and feminine chatter. Like its proprietress, the interior of the shop made a bold statement. Decorated in bright red, black and chrome, the place was trendy and fun, even though the majority of Donetta's customers were older ladies wanting a shampoo and set rather than the latest fad cut or color shown in the photos hanging on the walls of the salon.

Donetta was dressed in tight jeans that rode low on her hips, a pink cropped top that left her belly exposed, and platform shoes that added five inches to her height. Her flame-red hair was piled on her head in a messy up-do held in place by chopsticks. Only a self-assured woman could get away with the crazy style.

Sunny tapped the bell on the reception desk and everyone in the salon looked toward the front door.

A hush froze the moment.

A second later, Donetta dropped her bleach brush and squealed, leaving her customer with tinfoil sprouting from her hair. Tracy Lynn jumped out of the empty salon chair she'd been using to dab at her makeup, and Becca Sue sent a magazine sailing. The four of them met in the middle of the salon in a group hug.

"I can't believe you're back," Tracy Lynn said. "It'll be just like old times."

"Still double-booking your date calendar?" Sunny asked.

"Of course," Becca answered for her. "And she's still trying to pawn her leavings on to us."

Sunny stood back and looked at her friends. The Texas Sweethearts. They'd gone from childhood to braces to acne together, then to boyfriends and adulthood. Donetta ran a successful beauty salon where all the gossip was exchanged. Becca owned the quaint boutique down the street that sold books and coffee on one side and antiques, trinkets and gifts on the other. Tracy Lynn, former cheerleader, prom queen and Miss Hope Valley, spent her time on charities, spearheading programs to benefit newborn babies and the elderly and acting as hostess for her wealthy widowed father, the mayor.

"I've missed you guys," Sunny said. "And Becca, what are you doing off work in the middle of the day?" The youngest of the Sweethearts by six months—which she delighted in reminding them of—Becca loved to try new things. That was evident by her short, raven hair adorned with chunky streaks of maroon. "Who's minding your store?"

"Abbe Shea. You remember her, don't you? She transferred to Hope Valley High in our junior year."

Sunny nodded. "I remember."

"She moved back to Hope Valley last year. Teaches fifth grade, and since school's out for the summer, she's helping me at the store. She has a little girl now—Jolene. Cutest thing. Three years old."

"I didn't know Abbe got married."

Donetta tsked, but it was Tracy Lynn who answered. "Why do people think you have to be married to have a child? Honestly, Sunny. You've been in California for ten years. I'd expect you to be more with it."

The heat in Tracy's statement caused Sunny's brows to raise. She held up her hands in defense. "Darn. I've been here less than five minutes and already I have to hang my panties on Bertha."

There was a moment of silence, then they all

laughed, dissolving Tracy Lynn's strange mood. Bertha was a gnarled cottonwood on the banks of the lake. Hanging panties from the branches was a Texas Sweetheart ritual that took place whenever one of them did or said something beyond the pale.

Donetta went back to her customer and picked up where she'd left off, painting bleach solution on sections of hair and wrapping it in foil. Sunny didn't recognize the woman.

"If you're wearing a thong," Donetta said, "you'd better forget it. That brother of yours will have his deputies combing the area for sexual perverts."

"I doubt it. Storm knew about our ritual."

"He did not!" Donetta's mascara-enhanced lashes lifted to within a hairsbreadth of her red brows.

Sunny grinned. "Yes. And it was yours he saw. That time you went out with Tommy Drew when he was still dating Tracy."

"I didn't *know* she was still dating him." Donetta glanced at Tracy Lynn, who gave a wicked smile and fluffed her silky, straight blond hair.

Sunny shrugged. "Water under the bridge. Still, Storm saw you."

"How come you never told us?"

"He's my brother." In Sunny's opinion, that said it all. The four girls were as close as sisters. That made Storm an honorary brother to them all.

"How's Storm getting along?" Becca asked.

"Y'all would probably know that better than me. I just got into town this morning. I haven't seen him yet." Storm was an ex-Texas Ranger who'd been injured on the job. He'd come home to recuperate—at their mother's insistence—and ended up staying, quitting the Rangers and getting himself elected sheriff of Hope Valley.

"I'm glad to know you have your priorities straight," Donetta said, sitting in an unoccupied chair while her customer's hair processed. "Park yourself and bring us up-to-date on California gossip."

The salon boasted four domed hair dryers, four workstations and two shampoo bowls. A tiny reception desk stood at the front of the room and several red vinyl chairs lined the walls for customers or visitors to sit awhile and chat. Tracy Lynn was in one of the salon chairs, messing with her hair. Becca and Sunny dragged two guest chairs across the room and sat near her.

"California's pretty much the same."

"What Donetta meant," Tracy Lynn said, "is tell us about Michael."

"Nothing exciting there, either. Michael dumped me."

"You didn't say that when you called!" Donetta's green eyes narrowed. Of the four of them, she and Sunny were the closest. Their birthdays were a day apart. In fact, they'd both be turning thirty in a couple of months.

"I figured I'd wait and only have to spill my guts once. Having to admit you've been dumped is demoralizing enough."

Like true friends who didn't need to know details to automatically jump to her defense, each woman dutifully expressed contempt and good riddance.

"You hocked the ring, I hope," Becca said.

"He took it back."

"You're kidding!" Donetta exclaimed.

Everyone gasped, including the two ladies only halfway under the hair dryers and the one still in Donetta's chair. "What a jerk."

Sunny shrugged. "Michael was ever the frugal one. Besides, what do I need with a reminder?"

"The cash," Tracy Lynn said.

"I thought you said Michael was loaded." Donetta leaned forward in the chair, the glitter on her fingernails sparkling in the overhead light.

"Sure, he had money. That didn't mean he was willing to toss it around."

Tracy Lynn reached over and laid a hand on Sunny's arm. "Are you all right?" Her friend's compassion—not the loss of Michael—brought tears to Sunny's eyes.

"Yeah. I'm good. I think I've known for a while that Michael and I weren't right for each other. It's just you get in a pattern, you know? It's easier to stay in a nowhere relationship than to venture out and start over. It sounds stupid, but waking up each morning knowing I was part of a couple and had a date for Saturday night was easier than facing friends' questions and starting over again single."

She glanced at Donetta, knowing that she, of all the Texas Sweethearts, would understand. Donetta had stayed in a destructive marriage for two years before she'd found the strength to get out.

"I just wish *I'd* been the one who'd done the dumping," Sunny confessed.

"So, lie," Becca suggested with a grin.

"Wouldn't work. Turns out my elite friends were actually Michael's pals. His political standing in the community made him more attractive when it came down to choosing sides. In one day, I went from having a busy social schedule to having a calendar filled with cancellations.''

Donetta reached over and took her hand. Tracy Lynn and Becca laid theirs on top—another Texas Sweetheart ritual. Sunny's throat ached with suppressed sobs at the show of camaraderie.

''*We* would have never let you down that way,'' Donetta said quietly.

''I know,'' Sunny whispered. True friends.

Because of Jackson Slade's actions ten years ago, she'd left this town, these girlfriends; thought she'd wanted something so different. In moments like this she wondered what in the world she'd been thinking.

Not one to be left out if compassion needed doling out, Simba rested his head on their joined hands.

Sunny laughed, breaking the emotional silence. ''Let's get a grip here. I'm not pining for Michael. My pride's just smarting.''

''Yes, well, he should be hanged by his toenails for even doing that much to you,'' Tracy Lynn said.

''I'd have suggested another part of his anatomy,'' Becca muttered.

The door to the salon whooshed open and Simba whirled around, his tail slapping Becca, Tracy Lynn and Donetta with one wide sweep. Sunny grabbed his collar before he could lunge forward.

''Uh-oh,'' Donetta whispered. ''My favorite customer has arrived. She comes in every Friday for her shampoo, set and silver-blue rinse.''

Sunny recognized the woman immediately: Miz Millicent Lloyd. She hadn't changed a bit. The woman wore white gloves—which she wouldn't dare don a second before Easter Sunday—a belted silk dress that hung to her shins and open-toed shoes that matched the white pocketbook hanging from her arm.

Using a typical gesture Sunny well remembered, Miz Lloyd sniffed as though smelling something foul. In a cattle town, that wasn't such a stretch.

"I might have known you'd be in here, Rebecca Sue," Millicent said with an arch of one blue-tinted eyebrow. "I was of a mind to shop for a dear friend's anniversary gift, kill two birds, as I was in town to have my hair fixed. But no one was around to wait on me."

"Abbe's there," Becca said.

Mrs. Lloyd sniffed again. "She doesn't know my tastes. Besides, she has that...child with her. How's a person supposed to concentrate with a child running underfoot, I ask you?"

Tracy Lynn stopped primping and came out of the chair. Sunny hadn't been part of this town for a while, but she'd kept up in weekly letters. Tracy was a champion for any underdog, and had a soft spot for single mothers. Hadn't she nearly taken Sunny's head off over an innocent comment earlier?

Becca seemed to realize that Tracy Lynn was about to intervene. She had that shoulders-squared, country-club air about her, making her a fine match for the likes of Miz Millicent Lloyd.

"I was just headed back to the store, anyway," Becca said.

"A lot of good it'll do me now. It's time for my hairdo appoin—" She stopped midword, her eyes widening behind her glasses. "Well, I never, Donetta. When did you start allowing animals in your beauty shop? Aren't there health codes against that?"

Donetta opened her mouth, but Sunny cut her off.

"Hey, Miz Lloyd," she said. "It's nice to see you again."

The woman squinted behind her glasses. "Is that you, Sunny Leigh?"

"Yes, ma'am."

"Well then, I'm sure your mama taught you better manners than to bring your...animal to the beauty shop."

"Yes, ma'am. I'll just put Simba in the back. He was eager to see the girls."

Millicent Lloyd stared at Sunny as though she'd lost her mind. But there was no sense getting in a debate with the dowager. Folks rarely won against her.

Simba gave quick licks all around, then trotted across the salon with Sunny. Before she could close the break-room door, he realized he was being banished. His ears perked up and his velvety brown eyes beseeched.

"Don't look at me that way. I need you to be a good boy. Besides, I'm saving you a lot of grief. Miz Lloyd can ruin a mood faster than a flea can hop." Simba's ears lowered at that. "She's not as bad as she seems, though. She lost her husband some years back, and her attitude just hides her loneliness. You wouldn't know it from looking at her, but she has a big heart. When Daddy got sick, Miz Lloyd stepped right in and took over for Mama." Simba appeared happy with that explanation. "Lie down on the cool tiles there. And stay out of the refrigerator."

After closing the door, Sunny returned to the front of the salon. Millicent was already at the shampoo bowl, draped in a cape, and Donetta was rinsing her hair.

"Becca Sue went back to her store," Tracy Lynn

said, sweeping crimson gloss over her lips as she cut her gaze toward Millicent. "I told her we'd all get together after work."

"Sounds good to me," Sunny said, although she was starting to fade. She'd driven the last leg of the trip from California early this morning and was operating on precious little sleep.

She stood by Tracy Lynn as Donetta rolled curlers around Millicent's short gray hair—well, blue, actually—and dutifully listened to the older woman lamenting about the corns on her feet and how she was annoyed with a particular shoe company for discontinuing her favorite, open-toed style.

Sunny was nearly falling asleep when the glass door whooshed open again.

A hush fell over the salon, and Sunny's pulse jumped right up into her throat.

Jackson Slade stood in the doorway, the short sleeves of his white T-shirt rolled up in a bad-boy style that showed off his strong shoulders and biceps. As before, his tobacco-brown hat rode low on his forehead, shading his expression.

Tori, solemn and fragile, hugged his side, her hand wrapped in his. Sunny was struck again by how petite the nine-year-old was—especially next to a man as tall and commanding as Jack.

From the look on the faces of the two ladies sitting in the dryer chairs, they were scandalized at Jack's presence in their midst. Never mind that he was now a father and a successful rancher who was indirectly responsible for a good many jobs in Hope Valley. Memories ran long and deep in small towns. Some of the old-timers still thought of him as that drunkard Russell Slade's boy, a lad who belonged in reform school instead of in a booth in Wanda's Diner, slouching indolently and sipping on a cherry Coke among genteel society as though he belonged or something.

Ignoring the twittering old ladies, Sunny went to Jack and his daughter, her fatigue banished by an odd jolt of adrenaline.

"Tori's got gum in her hair," he said. "She didn't want me to cut it, so I figured I'd better bring her in."

The child looked frightened, as though she'd done something very wrong and anticipated dire consequences. But Jack didn't appear the least annoyed with his daughter. When he gazed at the little girl, a softness came over his face, as if she were the center of his world.

After checking for the snake—and feeling relieved to note that it was no longer around Tori's neck—Sunny bent to the child's level and ran her fingers over the wad of gum tangled in the long blond strands.

"Don't you just hate it when this happens?" she asked. "I did the same thing once, but my Grandma Birdie fixed me right up with a dab of peanut butter."

"Peanut butter?" Tori whispered.

"Yep. She smeared it on and the gum slid right out."

"And lucky for you," Donetta said, coming up beside Sunny, "I happen to keep a jar in the shampoo cupboard just for this sort of thing. We girls are forever getting stuff in our hair. Hey, Jack. How's it going?"

"Busy. I keep running out of hours in the day."

"You need to learn how to relax more."

Sunny stood and frowned. "How does relaxing give you more hours?" The logic didn't add up.

"Less stress," Donetta said. "You accomplish

more in the time allotted. You want me to trim that hair of yours some while you're here, Jack?''

He glanced at the ladies in the salon, who were still watching him as if he were a skunk who'd wandered in and they were hoping he'd wander back out.

"I'll pass, thanks. I have to run over to the feed shop and pick up some supplies.''

Sunny was glad he'd declined the haircut. She liked the longer style on him. As the light shifted against his hair, she caught a glint on his ear. A diamond earring. Sunny had given him a small gold hoop on their one-year-of-dating anniversary. Had his wife replaced the simple hoop with the more expensive diamond stud?

Ridiculously, it bothered Sunny, even though she knew good and well she shouldn't be dwelling on things that had to do with Jackson Slade's personal life.

The past needed to stay right where it was. In the past.

Sunny held out her hand to Tori. "Come on, sugar. Donetta's the best hairdresser there is. Let's us have a primping party while your daddy buys his feed.''

Jack ran his free hand over Tori's smooth cheek. "It's okay, darlin'. I'll only be across the street.''

Reluctantly, Tori let go of Jack's hand and took Sunny's.

For a moment, he stared at their joined fingers, then looked up at Sunny. She wondered what he was thinking. That if he hadn't screwed up, they could have had their own child together?

Her heart stung as though attacked by a swarm of angry wasps. Yes, this nine-year-old, blond-haired little girl could have been theirs. *Should* have been theirs.

But Jack hadn't loved Sunny enough.

He had chosen someone else.

Chapter Five

While Donetta styled the hair of the ladies who'd been under the dryers, and got them out the door, Sunny and Tracy Lynn decided to help out and wash Tori's hair.

The little girl, her head tipped back over a shampoo bowl, kept glancing toward the front door, then back at the relative strangers arguing over the peanut-butter jar and the temperature of the water.

"You're making a mess," Tracy said.

"Well, if you wouldn't hover, I'd have a little elbow room. I *know* how to wash hair."

"On animals, I suppose."

"I diagnose animals, I don't groom them."

"Well, there's a news flash. Look, you're getting water in this child's ear. Give me that squirter." Tracy Lynn won the battle, using her hip to bump Sunny out of the way.

The jolt sent the water hose slipping from Sunny's hand. It snaked wildly in the sink, drenching all three of them before anyone could get ahold of it. Tracy Lynn shrieked.

At the last second, Sunny had enough sense to shut off the tap. "Holy crud! What's the matter with you?"

Tori, momentarily stunned by all the water, suddenly blinked and let out a soft giggle.

Tracy Lynn and Sunny stopped glaring at each other, looked at the little girl and joined in the laughter.

"She always was the bossy one," Sunny said of Tracy. She was thrilled by Tori's show of emotion. The drenching had been worth it!

"And *she* was always hopeless with hair," Tracy Lynn countered. "All those glorious curls, and she just lets them go to frizz." She turned the faucet back on and expertly cascaded water over Tori's long hair, keeping the spray right at the hair line, as though there were an invisible barrier to prevent splashing in her eyes.

"This godawful humidity is making it frizz," Sunny said in defense of her hair.

"I could fix that," Donetta commented, eavesdropping on the chatter at the shampoo bowl. She emptied half a can of hair spray on Millicent Lloyd's hairdo, then patted the woman's shoulder and removed the protective cape. "All done, Miz Lloyd."

"And not a second too soon," the older woman said with a sniff. "A person comes in for a nice hairdo and nearly gets a shower bath." She moved over to the shampoo bowl where Tracy Lynn was massaging conditioner through Tori's hair. "That gum come out?"

"Good as new," Tracy Lynn said, letting Tori's wet hair sift through her fingers.

"Peanut butter." Millicent inspected the gum-free hair. "What will you kids think of next." Despite her gruff tone, she gave Tori's leg a pat, then extracted money from her pocketbook, handed it to Donetta and let herself out the door.

"Can Simba come and play now?" Sunny asked.

"You intend to practice with the water hose again?"

Sunny snorted in Tracy's direction and didn't bother to answer. Simba was happy to be set free, and ran into the front of the salon, glancing around to see what he'd missed.

Tracy Lynn had Tori sitting up, and was using a towel to blot her hair dry. After the first fifteen minutes, Tori had stopped looking toward the front door for her father to come back—proving that the Texas Sweethearts could win anyone over.

Simba went straight to them, inspected the goings-on and bathed Tori's leg with a quick lick.

The child giggled again.

"Simba," Sunny warned.

"It's okay," Tori said softly, a dimple flashing in her cheek. She scratched the dog's ears.

"Oh, now you've done it," Sunny said. "He'll be your friend for life."

That seemed to please Tori. "He looks like Scooby-Doo."

"Yes, he's been told that. Scooby-Doo, or the comic-strip dog Marmaduke. Both are famous, so Simba's a little conceited, if you want to know the truth."

"The real Simba's a lion," Tori pointed out.

Tracy and Donetta glanced at Sunny. They were all aware that the child was obviously coming out of her shyness a bit, talking more.

"And a lion's in the cat family," Sunny said promptly. Used to explaining why she'd chosen her dog's name, she covered Simba's ears, which elicited another giggle from the charming little girl. "The truth is, he can't seem to get it through his head that he's a dog and not a cat.''

Sunny let go of Simba's ears. ''Hop down and we'll get you settled in Donetta's chair. While she works her magic and fixes you up with a cool hairstyle, I'll tell you about how I found Simba.''

Tori scrambled down, then let Donetta help her into the salon chair. Simba followed dutifully and lay at her feet.

Donetta turned the blow dryer on low so Sunny didn't have to shout over the noise.

''I named him Simba because he was an abandoned puppy who was raised by cats. In California, they don't allow dogs to run around without a leash, and even as a puppy he was too big for someone not to notice him. So he got hauled to the pound and put in with the other dogs. And he was scared half to death. You see, he'd never looked in a mirror before, and since his family was feline, he must have thought he was just like them—at least, that's what the people at the pound thought.''

''Why in the world?'' Tracy Lynn asked, even though she knew the story. The question was for Tori's benefit, but Sunny didn't let on.

''Because somehow he'd managed to sneak out of his cage, and when one of the employees opened a door to a pen holding a litter of kittens, Simba jumped in and refused to come out.''

''Did they let him stay?'' Tori asked, her brown eyes wide, her mouth curved into a smile.

''Yep. And that's how I found him, this huge, silly-looking dog lying smack in the middle of a litter of kittens. So that's why I named him Simba. He's a big old pussycat.''

"We have a kitty. She's black, with a white dot on her nose." Tori glanced toward the reception desk. "I bet Simba would like Twinkie, don't you think, Daddy?"

Daddy?

Sunny sent an I'm-going-to-kill-you look at Donetta and Tracy Lynn—*they* were facing the door. Then she whipped around.

Jack was leaning against the reception desk, unabashedly listening to her tell Simba's life history.

"I imagine he would, darlin'," he said to his daughter, straightening away from the counter.

His eyes met Sunny's and her heart jumped. His expression was guarded, but she felt an agitation emanating from him like heat waves on hot asphalt. Her senses went on alert.

Stepping over Simba, she walked toward Jack. "What's up?"

He glanced beyond her shoulder to where Tori was happily gazing in the mirror as Donetta let her choose which glittery barrette she'd like in her hair. "Can I talk to you…outside?"

She nodded and opened the door. The heat hit her like a blast from a furnace.

"I—" He started to speak, then frowned at the front of her shirt. "What happened to you?"

She'd almost forgotten about her impromptu shower at the shampoo bowl. Looking down, she noticed the way the thin red cotton clung to the outline of her bra. "Tracy Lynn and I got into a water fight."

His brows rose beneath his Stetson, yet his gaze remained on her breasts.

She put a finger under his chin. "Polite folks talk face-to-face, cowboy."

His gaze lifted. It seemed to take a moment for him to gather his thoughts. Then his eyes cleared.

"I just got a call from the ranch. I've got another dead cow."

SUNNY WENT OUT to Jack's ranch for the second time that day. It was late afternoon, but the heat hadn't abated.

Beau grudgingly let Simba into the house to play with Tori, and Jack got into Sunny's SUV and rode out with her to where his foreman was standing guard over the dead animal.

"You told your man not to touch the cow, didn't you?" The Suburban lurched and bucked over the rutted ground as she cut across the field.

Jack was quiet. She glanced over at him, saw a muscle twitch in his jaw.

"Sorry," she said. "I asked that before, didn't I?"

His nod was terse. She understood his turmoil. No rancher wanted to think about an epidemic infecting his prize beef. It could wipe out his entire livelihood.

A man about Jack's age was leaning against a truck, smoking a cigarette. When they pulled up, he stubbed out the butt and met them halfway.

"This is Duane Keegan, my foreman," Jack said. "Duane, Sunny Carmichael. She's stepping in for Doc Levin."

"We can sure use you," Duane told her. He was at least a head shorter than Jack, with a pretty-boy face that would have been model perfect if not for the scar bisecting his chin. "I found this old gal about an hour ago." He gestured toward the cow lying motionless on her side, flies buzzing around like moths batting at a bright bulb. "Boss told me not to touch her, so I've just stood watch. Scotty and Junior came out and moved the rest of the herd.''

"Thanks, Duane," Jack said, stepping toward the dead cow.

Sunny stopped him with a hand on his arm. "Hang on a sec, will you?"

He seemed annoyed, but waited until she got her medical case out of the Suburban. Lamenting the heat, she donned a long-sleeved jumpsuit, tied a surgical mask around her face and pulled on a pair of latex gloves, then handed Jack gloves and a mask. "Let me do the handling, okay?"

"It's my property. My liability."

"And it's my expertise."

For a moment they engaged in a silent battle of wills. Then he nodded and put on the mask and gloves.

Squatting next to the animal, Sunny shooed away the tenacious flies and ran her hands and gaze over every inch of the cow. There was evidence of foaming saliva at the mouth, but the skin and eyes weren't jaundiced, and she could detect no unusual lesions. This cow almost appeared to have keeled over from a heart attack or heat stroke.

She glanced at Duane. "You found the first cow, I understand?"

"Yes, ma'am."

"'Sunny' will do." The closer she got to thirty, the more she hated anyone calling her "ma'am." "Jack said you mentioned lesions. What did they look like?"

Duane shrugged and lit another cigarette. "Just sores, I suppose. Could have been bites from a horsefly or something."

She noted that Jack's jaw was tight enough to snap,

knew he was wishing he'd been able to inspect that first cow himself.

She removed a kit from her case and gathered blood and tissue samples, then quickly sealed the smears so she could send them off to a lab for analysis. She needed better test kits, better tools of the trade, but since she'd been on vacation when her mother had phoned and this wasn't an official case, she hadn't felt comfortable raiding the lab for supplies. Most of the time when she went out on call, she worked out of a well-equipped mobile clinic. Right now, she was operating with the bare minimum.

"You've vaccinated for anthrax?" she asked Jack.

"Yes." He crouched beside her, watching every move she made. "On the Forked S we vaccinate for everything."

With a well-run cattle ranch like this one, she'd suspected as much. Jack wouldn't have been careless. She recognized the vaccination tattoos and tags.

"Have you added any new animals to your herd recently?"

"Not from outside sources."

She could tell he knew what she was asking. Foot-and-mouth disease wasn't a problem in the United States, but for ranchers and veterinarians alike, it raised horrible fears. She was ninety-nine percent certain that wasn't what they were dealing with here, since there were no signs of blisters in the mouth or on the hooves.

A myriad other diseases could wipe out a beef herd, though. That they were dealing with just two cows, that other stock from Jack's herd weren't dropping like weevils beneath a crop duster's spray, gave her hope.

She stood, having collected her samples as best she

could with what she had to work with. After removing her gloves, she double-bagged them and put them in her case.

"Have you noticed the cattle being off their feed lately? Appearing weak? Running fevers?"

"No." Jack pulled off his gloves and mask. "Tell me what you're thinking."

"I'd rather not speculate, Jack."

"I'm not going to panic."

"I never said you would."

He reached out to stop her from moving away, his palm connecting with the bare skin at her midriff where her top had ridden up. For a ridiculous moment, she imagined it was a lover's touch. Her body reacted in kind, her heart thumping, her breath catching in her lungs.

Endless moments passed as she stared into his blue eyes. When at last he dropped his hand, she didn't know whether to feel relieved or sorry.

She sighed. "There are just too many variables here, and I don't have the right equipment to make a diagnosis. We could be dealing with any number of things. Even if you're diligent about vaccination, that doesn't mean your neighbors are. Ticks and horn flies can spread disease from one herd to the next. I'll send these samples in and see what the lab says. Meanwhile, I have to check the rest of the herd—but I'll need supplies."

"I imagine there are supplies at Doc Levin's."

"My mom told me he'd up and left without a word. I thought he intended to stick around after he took over Dr. Porter's practice. Do you think he'll be back?"

"No one knows. Kat Durant is handling real estate

now. She'll have the keys to the clinic. No reason you can't step in and use his place.''

''I'll check it out. Might not be a bad idea to administer a dose of oxytetracycline to the whole herd. Do you use antibiotics in your feed?''

''No. I like to keep my beef as hormone-and-drug-free as possible.''

She nodded. Basically, Jack's cows were merely an early form of pot roast, raised to end up on someone's supper table.

''Could it be anaplasmosis?'' he asked.

A good rancher knew about infectious diseases. And ranching was Jack's lifeblood. ''Like I said, it's too early to speculate.''

''You mean, admit to your speculations.''

She shrugged. ''Whatever.'' Turning to Duane, who was standing off to the side smoking another cigarette, she said, ''Go ahead and burn this cow, and keep the rest of the herd clear of the area.'' She wasn't equipped to perform an autopsy, so disposing of the cow was the best option.

''Yes'm.''

Jack raised a brow at her taking charge, but signaled his agreement with a nod and walked back with her to the truck.

''You seem pretty good at what you do.''

''The government pays me to be good.''

''Will you be reporting this incident?''

She hated the thought of throwing the whole town into a tailspin. One leak to the media and the entire state would end up in mass hysteria. She was qualified to conduct the preliminary investigation. But that would require some sacrifices on Jack's part. Sacrifices he wasn't going to like.

"If you had a large number of your herd dying, I would definitely call in reinforcements. But this doesn't feel like an epidemic. There are several easily treatable conditions that can emulate infectious diseases. I'll know more when I get the lab results back on these specimens. In the meantime, I'd like to keep things low-key. I want your cattle quarantined, though. Until I make a diagnosis, you won't be selling your beef."

Although his jaw tightened, he nodded.

She laid a hand on his arm. "I'll be as thorough and fast as I can, Jack. It just has to be this way."

"I know. But time is money. Something like this could ruin me."

And though it wouldn't be her fault, she would be the instigator of that ruin if she ordered a mass slaughter of his beef. "I understand. I'm sorry."

He stared at her for a long time. His probing look made her squirm. Discreetly, she brushed at her face in case there was stray dirt—or God knows what else—on it, then finally gave in to the pressure. "What?"

"Just thinking."

"Well, do it out loud, okay? I'm starting to feel self-conscious."

The corner of his mouth twitched. "You've always loved animals. How come you didn't go for treating the cuddly kind?"

"Me? Cuddly animals? Look at my dog."

"I've been meaning to ask you about him."

"What?" Her shoulders straightened. She didn't sit still for anyone messing with Simba's psyche. On the off chance that Jack intended to insult him, she reached out to cover Simba's ears—then remembered she'd left him back at the ranch with Tori.

Jack opened his mouth, stared, then laughed.

"You're so used to that mutt being by your side, you forgot he wasn't."

She shrugged. "Simba's my pal."

"I heard you had another pal."

She glanced at him. "Michael?"

"Is Michael the fiancé?"

"Ex."

Jack's eyes bored into hers for another long moment, then he tipped his hat back on his forehead and nodded. "Guess that explains it."

"Explains what?"

"Why I keep seeing glimpses of vulnerability in your eyes. You're pining."

"I'm not pining for Michael."

"No?" He brushed a curl back from her forehead. "Then who?"

What in the world was going on here? It was as though he was asking about the two of them. But there hadn't been anything between them for ten long years. He'd seen to that.

"It's not you, if that's what you're thinking. That'd be ridiculous."

"Would it? Maybe I've been pining for *you.*"

She was so stunned by that statement the words that jumped into her brain were out before she could stop them. "Then why didn't you fight for me?"

"You're the one who left."

"What did you expect after I saw you playing kissy face with Lanette?"

"Did you ever stop to think you might have misunderstood what you saw?"

"A woman crawling all over my fiancé? Lips locked? Hands groping? Seemed pretty self-explanatory to me. Besides, if you thought there was a misunderstanding, you could have come after me, explained."

"Life's not a fairy tale, sugar bear."

Her stomach was twisted in knots so tight she wanted to scream. "God, you make me mad."

"Believe me, sugar, you haven't got *that* market cornered. And as far as coming after you, I didn't know where you were."

"That's a lame excuse. You could have asked."

"Right. Like you didn't swear everyone to secrecy. Your gal pals don't mind passing along gossip, but when it comes to you, they've got lockjaw."

"And my mother?"

He shrugged. "I asked once. She told me she had to respect what you'd told her in confidence. I never brought it up again."

"Then how'd you know about Michael? And get it in your mind that I was a scientist?"

"When I moved back to Hope Valley, Anna mentioned you a time or two."

Sunny didn't doubt that. Anna had made no bones about feeling that Sunny should have looked the other way ten years ago.

She glanced toward the horizon, where the sun was beginning to set. She should never have started this conversation. She had a new life, was a completely different person now. There wasn't any sense in rehashing the past. Jack had married Lanette and had a child with her. Misunderstanding or not, that was a pretty huge step for a man to take so soon after professing to love *her*.

"We've gotten off the subject," she said, tucking her medical case in the back of the Suburban and shutting the door. "I'll get ahold of Kat Durant tomorrow and check out Doc Levin's clinic, though I'm fairly certain he won't have the type of equipment I'll need."

She glanced at her watch. It was late afternoon in California, but that didn't really matter. Marty Zelweger practically lived at the lab. Chances were very good Sunny would catch him at no matter what time she called. She could trust Marty to be discreet.

"Let me make a quick call. I know a guy who can probably help us out."

She turned on her cell phone, pleased to see she had reception, and punched in the number of the lab.

Marty answered on the second ring.

"I figured you'd still be working," Sunny said, knowing she didn't need to identify herself.

"It's only four o'clock."

"Yes. And you've probably been there since four a.m. Listen, I need a favor. I'm in Texas, and I've got a situation with a couple of dead cattle."

"I thought you were on vacation, babe."

"You know me. I'm nearly as bad as you. Can't keep my fingers out of cow dung." She glanced at Jack, then turned her back to him as she explained the situation to Marty, detailing what she'd noted in her examination. "I'd like to keep this one quiet for a bit—it's in my hometown. I've got serum and tissue samples I'll overnight to you. In the meantime, what are the chances you can get me some decent lab supplies and test equipment?"

"It's doable, but you'll owe me three bags of jelly beans."

"I'll buy you ten." Marty loved his jelly beans. The expensive kind.

"In that case, I'll be your slave for life. Let's see. What I'm thinking isn't exactly in the George Washington code of honesty, but we'll work with it.... There's a supply lab in Houston. I can put in a will-call and have them hold the order instead of mailing it. I'll tell them you're on your way in from vacation and will pick it up."

"You're sure they'll release it?"

"I'll clear it. Just show your credentials. As far as I'm concerned, you're headed toward California. If you happen to double back to other parts of Texas because, say, you forgot your suitcase or something, I guess I wouldn't know that."

"You're a peach, Marty."

He sighed. "That's me. So when's some lady going to get smart and take a bite?"

"Probably when you get out of that office and socialize."

JACK LISTENED TO SUNNY as she laughed and spoke on the phone. The setting sun caught her hair and turned the curls a rich saffron. She was slimmer than he remembered, and with her back to him, his gaze naturally settled below her waist. Big mistake. His hands fairly itched to smooth over the curve of her derriere, where snug denim hugged her flesh like the skin on a nectarine. That was an itch he was *not* going to scratch.

Something that felt very close to jealousy gripped his gut and twisted when he noted how friendly she was with Marty. It was stupid, he knew, but that didn't loosen the knot in his stomach.

This had been a hell of a day. First, the jolt of Sunny showing up on his ranch after all these years; then, Tori's out-of-proportion reaction to getting gum in her hair; next, a second dead cow; and now, his annoyance over Sunny Carmichael having a simple, flirtatious phone conversation with another man. Hell, she was practically a stranger. What should he care whom she laughed with on the phone?

She had a life in California, a life he wasn't part of. Just because she was back in Hope Valley for a while didn't mean he had any claims on her.

The direction of his thoughts made him pause. Did he want a claim on her? Ten years had passed. He'd never forgotten her, never really gotten over her.

But she wasn't a woman he could trust.

When the going got tough, Sunny ran. He had a daughter to think about now. He couldn't chance letting Tori get close to another woman who didn't have sticking power, who might abandon her as her mother had.

And, damn it, he was getting way ahead of himself here. Sunny had only been back for a day. It just went to show what a powerful effect she had on him.

One day, and he was already thinking about the future.

Chapter Six

Sunny got up early the next morning and drove to Houston. She was authorized to use all the supplies and equipment she picked up, but the trip made her a nervous wreck because she wasn't exactly following procedure.

Unused to bending the rules, she felt as though she had guilt written in neon letters across her forehead.

Oh, sure, this was for the good of the community, the economy, the *government*. When it came right down to it, though, she had to admit she'd gone out on a limb for Jack.

Unrequited love. It was the pits.

She was back by noon, and when she walked into her mother's house, Mama was cooking—one of the things she did best.

The smells of fried okra, ham and corn bread filled the air, and Sunny's stomach rumbled. Simba, who was happily lapping up any morsel dropped on the floor, leaped over a dish of water, his hind leg not quite clearing it, and ran to Sunny.

"Oh, for heaven's sake. That dog is entirely too big to be indoors." Anna stooped to mop up the spilled water. "Did you finish your errands, dear?"

"Yes. Here, Mama. Let me do that." Sunny scratched Simba's ears, then started to grab a roll of paper towels.

"I've got it," Anna said, sending Simba a wry look that nevertheless revealed she was crazy about the huge animal. "Honestly, though, I can't see what was so important that you had to take off at the crack of dawn." She tossed the dishrag on the countertop, pulled out a pan of corn bread from the oven and set it on a hot pad. "I imagine Jack could have used your expertise out at his ranch, instead of you running all over creation. Ranchers start their day early, you know."

"I was running all over creation for *him*."

"Oh?" Anna set out three plates on the drop-leaf kitchen table. "Then I'm sure he'll be pleased. He's such a nice man. You'd do well to take a good look at that while you're here."

"Jack and I are history, Mama. You know that."

"Only because of your stubbornness."

Sunny wanted to scream. Instead, she breathed deep. "I can't change what happened ten years ago. But I have a life now. I'm highly respected in my field. I'm here only because you asked me to come and I had vacation time accumulated."

"And you were upset over Michael. In times like these you need your family. Sit. We'll have something to eat. Home is where you come when you need a pair of arms to comfort you, or some help putting meat on your bones."

Sunny sighed. One minute her mother was dismissing her career and the next was making her feel cherished. Sunny and her mom might not see eye-to-eye on a lot of things, but love wasn't one of them. She just wished…well, she didn't know what she wished for. Friendship on an adult level, perhaps. Fewer lectures.

How her mother kept working Jack into the conversation, subtly pushing, grated on Sunny's nerves. She was tired. She'd been traveling. And her emotions were plenty stirred up over Jackson Slade without any help whatsoever from Anna Carmichael.

"I don't need any more meat on my bones. And why have you set three places?"

"Because she's expecting her favorite son."

Sunny whirled around and grinned. "Storm!" Her brother stood in the doorway, wearing his khaki sheriff's uniform. She raced over and leaped into his arms, nearly tripping over Simba, who was determined not to be left out.

"You're her *only* son, you idiot. I might have known you'd be here to mooch a meal. Did Wanda's Diner close up or something?"

"Wanda's is great. But no one beats Mama's cooking." He hugged her a little tighter, then let go and leaned down to give Simba a scratch. The dog gave a quick lick and looked away. "I don't suppose you've taught this miniature horse any guard-dog talents other than licking yet?"

"I don't have to teach him anything. One look at his size and people cross the street and give me plenty of room."

He gave Simba another pat, then placed a kiss on Anna's cheek and sat at the table. "Thanks for the invitation, Mama."

Anna clucked around him, serving his dinner and filling his glass with iced tea. "You know you don't need an invitation to come home for a meal. I've always got a pot of something on the stove. And you have to take care of yourself, keep up your strength.''

Mama catered to Storm, Sunny noted. The way she'd catered to Daddy. Anna definitely treated men differently from women. They got the choicest piece of meat, were served first, coddled because they worked so hard.

Of course, Sunny understood the underlying worry her mother displayed over Storm. After he'd been shot several years ago while on duty as a Texas Ranger they all counted their blessings that he was even here to fuss over.

Her brother helped himself to a slice of corn bread and a slab of ham. ''See there? I'm not mooching. Mama recognizes that being the sheriff is hard work.''

Sunny rolled her eyes. ''Yeah, hard fending off all the ladies speeding through town just so you'll stop them and they can bribe you out of giving them a ticket.''

Storm's brows lifted. Where Sunny was fair like their mother, Storm had the dark, handsome features of their father. ''*Bribe*'s a pretty strong word, Pip.''

The nickname, short for pip-squeak, made her insides soften. She'd nearly lost this guy. She couldn't imagine life without him. Having Daddy gone was bad enough. Losing Storm would have been intolerable.

She reached for the bowl of okra and spooned the fried vegetable onto her plate. ''I probably work harder than you do. You've got a cushy, air-conditioned car you ride around in all day, hang out at the diner, have ladies bring you casseroles. I'm out in the middle of hot dusty corrals probing in cow orifices.''

"Nice dinner-table conversation," Storm said with a grin. "You're jealous 'cause Mom loves me best."

Sunny laughed, realizing he had no idea how that remark had cut. He didn't see it. "Don't be so sure, *Stormie.* She cooked for me, too."

"You two stop picking at each other and eat," Anna said, touching each of them gently on the shoulder before she rounded the table and sat down, a pleased expression on her face as she watched her children enjoy a meal.

Anna was a toucher. She could deliver disapproval and unasked-for advice as though it were her due, yet she petted, brushed, stroked or squeezed during the deliverance and at every other opportunity. It was an unconscious trait—sort of like Simba's walk-by lickings.

"I hear Slade found another dead cow," Storm commented, sipping his iced tea.

Sunny's brows drew together. "How'd you hear that?"

His eyes shot to Anna, who was overly busy buttering a slice of corn bread.

Naturally. "I'd just as soon keep this quiet until I've had a chance to investigate," Sunny said.

Storm nodded. "I understand. From my standpoint, I don't want to deal with a horde of media if there's nothing to it."

"My thought exactly," Anna said. "That's why I've kept talk of it within the family."

"Can't control what Slade's employees do, though," Storm said. "I couldn't really blame them if they got spooked and spread the word, in which case a media circus would be a given."

"I asked Jack to have a talk with his men. He feels

certain they're loyal.'' Sunny hoped that was the case—at least until she got a better handle on things. The supplies she'd picked up that morning would go a long way toward speeding up her job. ''No one wants to see Hope Valley tagged with the stigma of infected cattle.''

Storm looked across the table at her. ''How are you doing?'' he asked quietly.

She knew what he was asking. Unlike their mother, Storm had taken Sunny's side ten years ago. To keep him from paying Jack a visit with his fists had required all her persuasive skills. He would wonder now if it bothered her to be working closely with Jack.

''I'm good. Time heals, you know?''

He gave her an odd look. ''Mom said you're not with Michael anymore.''

Michael? Damn it, she'd nearly forgotten about him. Why had she automatically assumed Storm was subtly probing with regard to *Jack?*

''Guess she didn't leave us much to catch up on, hmm?''

Anna reached over and put a hand on Sunny's arm. ''Your brother would want to know these things.''

''I know, Mama. I wasn't criticizing.'' After all, Anna hadn't told Donetta, Becca or Tracy Lynn about the breakup. She was good at keeping things to herself when it counted. However…

''Since we're speaking of passing along information, you could have warned me that Jack wasn't even aware I was coming to town or why.''

''Men's egos are so fragile, Sunny. We wouldn't want him to think we were butting into his business.''

Sunny nearly choked on a swallow of iced tea. ''You crack me up, Mama.''

Anna folded her arms. "I'm glad I can provide you with entertainment."

If not for the pleased spark in her mother's eyes, Sunny might have thought she'd hurt her feelings. And she would never deliberately do that. Sunny knew what it was to wear your emotions on your sleeve. "Well, that's exactly what you did. Butted into his business. You also didn't tell me Jack's wife had died."

"Surely I did. I told you just yesterday she wasn't there."

"But not that she was gone *forever!*"

"Well, it's not polite to discuss the deceased."

Storm looked up from his plate, but clearly wasn't about to get in the middle of this conversation.

"Besides," Anna continued, helping herself to a slice of ham, "Lanette had already run off, abandoned her sweet child and served Jack with papers. They'd been divorced more than two years before he got the call about her dying. Did the decent thing, too, and paid for her burial."

So much for not talking about the deceased, Sunny thought. She moved her glass back and forth over the table, smearing the circle of water where the glass had sweated. She'd known Jack had gotten married, and she'd known he'd moved his family back to Hope Valley three years ago.

Would she have made an effort to come home for an extended visit if she'd known Lanette was no longer around?

It was one thing to run into an ex when he was committed to another woman. It was a different thing altogether if he was a free agent.

Sunny considered she'd done well for herself over

the years. The urge to show that to a man who'd thrown her away was something she figured was pretty universal. Most women would gain a certain satisfaction from flaunting their successes, and Sunny was no exception.

She'd enjoyed impressing Jack with her skill as a veterinarian yesterday. Had liked catching those long, curious looks when he didn't think she was watching.

Did he regret letting her go? Wonder what might have been?

This line of thinking was getting her nowhere. He'd hurt her. Etched scars on her soul that had yet to heal. The first couple of years had been devastatingly hard. She hadn't known a person could suffer so horribly, and for so long. Thankfully, she'd had school to distract her, but the agonizing pain of betrayal had constantly lurked below the surface like a raw wound that refused to heal.

Because she'd lost the man she'd been so certain was her soul mate.

Eventually, she'd mastered her emotions, put them into perspective. Yet she'd measured every man's actions by Jack's, had erected a wall around her heart. Even with Michael.

And Jack Slade was the last person she could allow to pierce the wall. *He'd* laid the first brick.

She glanced at the rooster clock over the sink. Time was ticking away, and she should be back out at the Forked S. The sooner she got to the bottom of things, the sooner she could concentrate on herself and the direction of her life.

As though reading her mind, Anna asked, "Will you be going to see to Jack's cattle this afternoon?"

"As soon as I get my things together."

"What time shall I expect you back?"

The circle of water on the table grew larger. Blotting it with her napkin, Sunny lifted her eyes. "Um, I won't be home tonight. I'm going to go stay at the Forked S."

Anna gave her a look that only a mother could. Disapproval fairly ricocheted around the room. "Stay, as in move in?"

"It makes sense. I've got a lot of work to do, and time is critical."

"But moving in with an unmarried man, Sunny?" She was clearly scandalized. "Good girls don't go living with men."

The minute Anna said the words she seemed to regret them. Sunny had practically lived with Michael. It hadn't been a full-time arrangement, but close.

"I meant here in Hope Valley. Things are different here. Besides, you're barely back in town. We've not had a chance to visit."

"I'm here to see about a cattle problem," Sunny reminded her. "Wasn't that the purpose of your call?"

"Yes. But that doesn't mean you have to *live* with the man. Or that you can't spend time with your mother and your family."

"It's not as though I'm going across the state line. I'll just be up the road at the Slade ranch."

"Well, I guess you figure that since you're nearing thirty you don't need to listen to your mother or worry about what others think."

"I try not to worry about what others think." *That's your department.* Her mother's attitude hurt, though Sunny should have been used to it. Anna had been preaching her what-will-the-neighbors-think speech ever since Sunny and Storm were babies. Storm ignored it. Sunny felt the words like little drips of acid on her heart. For once she wanted to be loved enough, to be considered important enough, that it didn't *matter* what the neighbors thought.

"I'd better get going. Like I said, I've got a lot of work to do."

"You'll come back for dinner?"

"I'll call." She leaned down and gave Storm a kiss on the cheek, then did the same for her mother. "You know, Mama, it works two ways. You can drive over to the ranch to see *me,* too."

JACK WAS JUST COMING OUT of the house when Sunny pulled up in the drive and got out of the Suburban, Simba leaping down beside her.

He'd been expecting her.

He *hadn't* been expecting the suitcase she hauled out of the back seat.

She walked up to him, her blond hair pulled back in a ponytail, her cheeks already slick with perspiration from the heat. Her chin lifted as she stopped in front of him, noticed that his gaze was on the suitcase.

"Are you going to give me a hard time about this, as well?"

"Can't very well give you a hard time, sugar b—sugar, if I don't know what *this* is." Simba nudged his palm and he obliged the huge dog, scratching his ears.

"I decided it would be expedient if I came out here to stay while I'm conducting my examination. The sooner I get it done, the sooner I'll be out of your hair and you can get your beef to market."

"I'm all for expediency."

She glared at him as though she expected him to

contradict her. Must have run into some opposition from her family, he figured.

"Want me to take that for you?" He nodded toward her suitcase.

"Just point me toward the bunkhouse and I'll handle it from there."

"You're not staying in the bunkhouse, Sunny."

"I don't mind."

"Well, I do. I'd get precious little work out of the men if they had to try to sleep while having a woman bunking in with them."

He took the suitcase from her and went back into the house, where he led the way up the stairs. Simba nearly knocked him over, racing ahead of them as though he had a personal invitation. They'd soon see how well Twinkie got along with a horse-size dog who thought he was a cat.

Cora came out of Tori's room with an armload of linens. Simba trotted right past her, sneaking a lick on her elbow without stopping.

"Goodness! Mind the cat, Tori," Cora called. "There's a dog on the loose."

"Sunny will be staying with us for a while, Cora," Jack stated.

"Oh. Well, that's lovely." Clearly, she couldn't wait to phone Anna and get the story. Anna and Cora were as close as kin, had been since they were girls in grade school.

When he heard his daughter's delighted shriek, he paused at her door. Tori was happily introducing the cat to Simba. Twinkie wasn't at all sure about the intruder, but Simba vibrated all over, his tail wagging, a silly canine grin on his mug, as if he'd just found a long-lost member of his family.

Jack felt his heart soften. Seeing his daughter smile, show some spark, was a relief. Sometimes he thought she was just too *good* for her own good. She was excruciatingly polite, soft-spoken, went out of her way to be helpful—as though she was striving for perfection.

Nine-year-old little girls should be full of mischief and fun.

"Hey, kiddo."

Tori stopped trying to corral the cat, and looked up. "Hi, Daddy. Twinkie's not being very sociable."

"Cats are conditioned to be fearful of dogs."

Tori covered Simba's ears—evidently, the way she'd seen Sunny do. "Simba's not a regular dog. Twinkie has to know that."

"Give her a little time, sweetie," Sunny said. "Simba, lie down now." The dog immediately plopped onto the oval braided rug. "That's a good boy. You be sweet and let Twinkie come to you in her own time." Simba's ears lowered, and he laid his nose on his front paws, his brown eyes going from Tori to Twinkie, then back to Sunny.

Tori giggled and looped an arm around Simba's neck, snuggling with the huge dog. "Are you here for a visit, Sunny?"

"Actually," Jack said, "Sunny and Simba will be staying with us for a bit."

"I'm going to take care of your daddy's cattle."

Tori sat on the floor, legs crossed, a hand-held electronic game beside her. "You're a veterinarian, aren't you?"

"That's right."

"What happens when somebody brings you a sick snake?"

Jack saw Sunny's eyes cut toward the terrarium, where the garter snake slept in a small rock cave. "Um, I haven't really had to deal with snakes on the job. When I was in school and worked at an animal clinic, I usually let one of the other doctors handle the snakes."

"But what if Gordie got sick and there was nobody else to take care of him?"

"Gordie is your snake?"

"Yes."

"Well, let's hope he doesn't get sick. Snakes are pretty hardy, anyway."

"But what if he did? Would you be scared of him?"

"Honestly? Yes, I'd be afraid of him. But I'd find a way to help him."

Tori nodded and turned her attention to Simba, who was quivering with ecstasy.

Jack liked Sunny's honesty, and the fact that she didn't talk down to his daughter.

"I'm going to put Sunny's things in the guest room, then we'll be out working with the cattle," he told the child. "If you need me…"

"I know, Daddy. I'll call the barn." She sounded so perfectly agreeable, rather than put out the way most kids her age would be when faced with an over-protective parent. Jack sighed. He wished he knew what had happened to his daughter's sparkle, couldn't help but wonder if he was doing something wrong.

"Can Simba stay in my room and play?"

"Sure, if he wants to."

"Cora said we could make cookies in a while if Beau will get out of the kitchen," Tori said. "Simba can help."

Jack laughed. "I imagine Beau will want to supervise. Be sure to save me a cookie, okay?"

He automatically put his hand out to escort Sunny farther down the hall, his palm connecting with the small of her back. Her skin was warm through the cotton T-shirt, and he felt the heat shoot straight up his arm.

Hell, if he reacted to an innocent touch, how was he going to survive seeing her walk his halls in her pajamas?

Annoyed with himself, he went into the yellow room and set the suitcase on the bed. "This used to be my brother Linc's room. Cora had a hand in redecorating it. She said yellow was a good color for a guest room."

"Where is Linc now?"

"Breeding horses over in Dallas."

"Do you keep in touch?"

"Couple of times a year. He likes being an uncle to Tori." Jack watched as Sunny wandered around the room, running her hand over the daisy-patterned quilt on the queensize, iron-rail bed.

"This is beautiful."

"My mom quilted it."

Sunny touched a gold-framed photograph of his mother that sat on the nightstand, then stooped to smell the fresh roses in a cobalt-blue vase. "She was a great woman. I always envied her green thumb. She had the most beautiful garden."

The mention of his mother brought a wave of sadness to Jack. Doris Slade had been a saint in his eyes. And he still missed her, still held his father responsible for her death. "Yeah, she was great."

"Did these come from your mom's garden?" Her fingers caressed a delicate yellow rose petal.

"Yes."

"I noticed it's still flourishing. Who keeps it up?"

"I do."

She looked at him as though he'd told her the sky was green.

"Is that so hard to believe?"

She shrugged. "You just don't seem the type to fuss with flowers."

"My masculinity's healthy enough."

Sunny's hand jerked, nearly knocking over the vase. She glanced at him and found she couldn't hold his gaze. Yes, his masculinity was definitely healthy. *Too* healthy, if her pounding heart and sweaty palms were any indication. It was as though he was taunting her, seeing if she'd react.

She swallowed hard when he moved across the room, coming straight for her. He was so close she could see the shadow of stubble on his cheeks and chin, the vein that pulsed at his temple, the tiny scar near his eyebrow where the branch of a tree had caught him when they'd been out horseback riding the summer she'd graduated from high school.

She looked up into his pale blue eyes, eyes that stood out against the deep walnut of his brows and hair. Time seemed to stand still. She felt as though she was caught in a storm and chaos swirled around her, yet here, right in the center of the tempest, was an eerie calm, a surreal cocoon of sensuality.

His lips were so close. His gaze rested on her hair, her eyes, her mouth. Unconsciously, she leaned forward, pulled against her will as if by a gravitational tug. So many years had gone by since she'd felt his mouth on hers, given herself over to this man, his strong arms, his skillful touch.

Yet the kiss she'd expected never came. He reached past her and flicked a switch on the wall.

Sunny blinked.

"The light plug," he said. "Now when you hit the switch by the door, the lamp will come on. You won't have to stumble in the dark."

He stepped back and she let out a breath. She felt like a fool. A raging mass of hormones. What in the world was she thinking?

"Thank you. I probably would have figured that out." She skirted around him, opened her suitcase and took out a baseball hat. "We'd better get started. I've got supplies in my Suburban."

"Sunny—"

She held up a hand, annoyed because she knew her disappointment and yearning had been written all over her face. "Look, Jack. Let's stick to business, okay? We've got a big job to do, and time's important."

"You wanted me to kiss you just now."

She looked straight at him, didn't bother to deny what was obvious. Using a variation of Jack's earlier words, she said, "My femininity's healthy enough. Let's leave it at that, okay?"

Chapter Seven

Jack grabbed the hose and ran water over his head and neck. He was hot and dusty. After that odd moment earlier in the bedroom, he and Sunny had been wary of each other, but duty soon took precedence.

She'd worked like a demon right beside him all afternoon, shoving annoyed cattle into makeshift chutes, sitting on calves to draw blood samples and inject vaccinations. They'd both earned a break.

Letting the water hose run in the trough, he glanced over at Sunny. She'd wiped her forehead with her arm, leaving behind a smear of dirt. Her curly hair, once shoved beneath a baseball cap, had long ago escaped, and cascaded around the shoulders of her long-sleeved, green cotton shirt. The seat and knees of her jeans were covered with dirt.

And damned if she didn't look good enough to pose for a layout in a ranch magazine.

"Want a splash?" he asked, holding the water aloft.

She gave him a mock glare and peeled off her suede gloves. "I found out yesterday I'm a little dangerous with water hoses."

He grinned, remembering her wet shirtfront at the salon. "I'll hold it for you."

"As if I'd trust you not to make me look like a contestant in a wet T-shirt contest."

That he'd want to see. He took a bandanna from around his neck and doused it with water, then shut off the hose and went over to her.

"Ye of little trust. You've got a smear of brown on your face. I'd hate to speculate on what it is." He touched the wet cloth to her cheek, watched her eyes widen in surprise, then close in utter appreciation.

The exquisite expression nearly made him groan. He paused for a moment and her eyes popped open.

"Feel good?" He had to clear his throat to speak.

She seemed to realize the intimacy of the act and sidestepped, taking the bandanna from his hand. "Thanks, I—I'll get it from here."

Finding himself more drawn to her than he'd like, Jack looked out over the ranch. The men had done a good job moving the herd and setting up temporary corrals, but they had a long way to go. This wasn't going to be a one-day operation.

Sunny had been thorough, as well, which had slowed the process. She'd visually inspected each cow, drawn blood, and together they'd worked out a system of collecting samples and cross-referencing with a special tag on each animal's ear.

"When will your friend have the lab results from what you gathered yesterday?"

"I told Marty to put a rush on it. Should be a day or two. It'll require a bit more time for these new samples, though, because of the volume."

And until then, he couldn't sell his beef.

Even if they didn't get a firm diagnosis on the dead cow, Jack couldn't chance having a single one of his cattle carrying disease. The economic repercussions were too risky, involved too many sectors.

Sunny handed him back his bandanna and he looped the damp scarf around his neck, which helped to cool him off. The humidity was worse today. From the look of the sky, they were due for a storm. Rain would turn this pasture into one hell of a mud puddle.

"The guys have been slowly parking the herd closer to the ranch. I think tomorrow we'll run them through the chute shed."

She glanced at the sky. "Probably be a good idea. I'll be glad for the rain to cool things off, but I'm not crazy about rolling around in muck. Cows in mud are just as slippery as pigs."

Jack leaned a hip against the trough. "You wrestled many slippery pigs?"

"You ought to remember. I beat your time by forty-five seconds at the Founder's Day competition. Remember?"

"Yeah," he said slowly. "I remember." And he remembered showering with her afterward, taking his time with the soap as he washed every bit of mud off of her.

Not two weeks later, she'd left town without a backward glance—without giving him a chance to offer an explanation for the damning scene she'd walked in on between Lanette and him.

He straightened away from the trough, annoyed with himself for inadvertently bringing up the past, for allowing the memories to surface. Other than his mother, Sunny had been the only woman he'd ever truly given his heart to—and she'd tossed it back without ever saying goodbye.

"I think we can call it a day. Beau and Cora will have supper ready pretty soon."

SUNNY NODDED AND FELL in beside him as he headed for the house. Keeping up with Jack's moods was hard. One minute he'd tease and the next he'd turn into a silent bear.

And darn it all, his stride was hard to keep up with as well. He was practically running, as though his tolerance for civil behavior was at an end.

After a day of strong-arming cows, Sunny wasn't up for a foot race.

Perhaps reminding him of the pig wrestling hadn't been such a good idea. "Would you slow down? I know I smell, but you're not exactly a sweet rose yourself."

He glared at her, but did slow his steps. She could see a muscle working in his jaw, the coiled strength in his arms. As a teen, he'd been known to brood—a modern-day James Dean, the bad boy with a chip on his shoulder. But with her, he'd learned to laugh, to lighten up.

She didn't like it when he went all lockjawed like this.

"It's going to be a long two weeks if we keep this up," she said.

"Keep what up?"

"This seesaw relationship. Why don't we just get what's between us out in the open and quit tiptoeing around? We had a past together—"

"Have. We *have* a past."

"Whatever. It's over. But memories are bound to crop up. Let's try to be friends so we can get through the examination of your cattle and prevent whatever happened to those two cows from happening to the rest of the herd.''

''Do you believe that's possible? For us to be friends?''

''Anything's possible if you set your mind to it.''

He stopped then and wrapped his hands around her upper arms. It was the first time he'd deliberately touched her since she'd come back. Her nerves skittered, and her breath stalled.

''When I look at you, I'm not thinking about friendship.''

Oh, man. Her heart was pounding in earnest now. A smart woman would run. Evidently, her brain cells had fried in the sun, because she whispered, ''What do you think about?''

He stepped behind a shed, nearly sweeping her off her feet as he dragged her with him. ''That there's something else we ought to get out of the way.''

When his lips came down on hers, her first instinct was to struggle. But emotions surfaced quickly, the past superseding the present. For a moment, she was transported back ten years. She knew this man's touch, his kiss. Knew the strength of his hands and how quickly the fire in him could ignite—sending her up in flames, as well.

He tasted of salt, cool water and masculinity. The brim of his hat grazed her cheek as he pushed his fingers through her hair to angle the kiss deeper, knocking off her baseball cap.

The feel of the cap slipping brought her to her senses.

She tugged back, breathing hard. ''Whoa. That's not part of the rules.''

His chest was rising and falling as fast as hers, yet

his voice was utterly controlled. "I wasn't aware there were rules."

"There are always rules."

"I'm a man who likes to break rules, sugar bear. You ought to know that."

Yes, she did, and hearing him say the words sent a thrill through her that was entirely inappropriate.

Still, he wasn't the only sinner standing out here in the heat. She herself had broken a few rules by going to Houston to get supplies for this cattle diagnosis.

She'd also just broken a major one by letting Jackson Slade kiss her.

"In our case, I think it would be wise to, um, not break them. Anymore. For the time being." Now she was babbling....

She took a breath. "I'm only here for a short while, Jack. Let's not complicate things."

He watched her for a long time, his hands clenched at his sides. "Sugar bear, your mere presence complicates things."

With that, he turned and strode toward the house, yanked open the back door and let it slam behind him. Hopefully, Beau wasn't fixing a soufflé for supper.

For a moment, Sunny stood in the fading sunlight, wondering if she should just head for her car and go back to her mother's.

Being in close quarters with Jack definitely complicated matters.

But the clock was ticking. She had less than three weeks of vacation left. After that, she'd either have to return to California or file an official report so she could stay here legitimately, make this official business.

But that wouldn't work, either. She just remembered

that three weeks from now she'd be at a veterinarians' convention in Washington, D.C., teaching a seminar on diagnostic procedures.

You're the only one we can trust, Sunny Leigh.

Her mother's words came back to her. It was important to prove herself, not let down her mother or this town.

Or Jack.

Sunny sighed and started for the back door. If she didn't turn up answers in the next couple of weeks, the Forked S was going to be scrutinized by the Department of Agriculture. And in all likelihood, they would send George Lansing to assist.

Sunny and George didn't get along. He was one of those slick, charming men who hated women. Especially women in power. She knew he wanted her job. If he found out she'd been conducting the investigation on her own, had used government equipment when she was technically on vacation, he'd make a mess of trouble for her.

He was also just cocky enough to quarantine the entire town and every ranch within a hundred-mile radius. She'd seen that sort of thing happen before, knew what it could do to the local economy. No one was allowed in, not even to drive through.

Extreme measures like that caused people to panic—and the media to swarm. Hope Valley would be stigmatized forever.

She needed to be here at Jack's ranch, where she was on hand to check anything that cropped up. She'd just have to make a better effort to keep distance between them, to watch her words and stick to business. No more trips down memory lane over pig wrestling. And no more fiery kisses.

SUNNY WANTED NOTHING MORE than to relax in a hot bath. Her body ached in places she hadn't known it could. Usually, she didn't get quite as physically involved in chasing down cattle as she had today. But Jack's crew was limited, since several of the men were still out rounding up the herd and sectioning off the stock she'd already checked and tagged.

She lowered herself into the tubful of silky bubbles and eased back against the porcelain rim. That kiss by the shed hadn't help matters, either. Her nerves were strung so tight she felt like a rubber band about to snap.

Pleading exhaustion, she'd skipped dinner with Jack and Tori and the ranch hands. Beau hadn't been pleased, but he'd been a good sport and shooed her upstairs after thrusting a roast-beef sandwich and a glass of tea into her hands.

Simba was thoroughly enamored with Tori, and Sunny felt a tad abandoned by her pet. But the sweet smile on the little girl's face was worth loaning out her dog for a while. Tori was determined that Simba and Twinkie become friends. Simba was all for the relationship; Twinkie, however, was still tentative.

The spicy scent of the bath gel lulled her. Just when she was almost totally relaxed, someone knocked on the bathroom door.

Adrenaline shot through her. Her heart slammed against her ribs. "Um...I'm in the tub."

She heard a mumble: Jack's voice. She couldn't make out his words. She glanced at the bubbles. They covered her. Not that it made any difference, since the door was closed.

"What? I can't hear what you're saying."

The door opened slowly and she forgot to breathe.

Used to living on her own most of the time, she rarely locked bathroom doors. Still, she wasn't accustomed to having her privacy breached. She snatched up a towel and covered herself. It immediately absorbed water and clung to her curves like a terry-cloth body mold.

Jack moved just far enough into the bathroom to talk to her, keeping his gaze focused on the mirror instead of her. She could see his reflection, and knew he could see hers. At one time, he'd seen all of her there was to see. But that had been a long time ago.

"For heaven's sa—"

"I just got a call from the barn. One of my mares is about to foal."

Sunny automatically sat up, sloshing water, forgetting about modesty. She held the wet towel to her front, but her back was exposed. "Is it a problem birth?"

"Scotty doesn't think so. Still, I'd feel better if you'd come out and stand by. This is her first foal."

"I'll be right there."

Jack closed the door and she scrambled out of the tub, wiping off bubbles, leaving wet footprints on the floor mat as she reached for a dry towel to wrap around herself. With her hair still pinned up, she raced into her room and dressed quickly, then rushed outside to the barn.

Jack was already there with Tori, who looked as though she'd been woken up.

"It's going to be Tori's foal," Jack said. "I thought she'd like to watch."

"Great idea. What's your mare's name, Tori?"

"Violet."

Sunny saw that the horse was lying down. Good.

Some were stubborn and wouldn't settle. "Well, Violet seems pretty relaxed at the moment, but we'll want to be quiet. If she gets agitated, don't feel bad if I ask you to go hide, okay? Some new mamas get nervous when there's a crowd of people."

Tori nodded. "Simba wanted to come, but Daddy said no."

"Don't let Simba's sulking put you on a guilt trip. He thinks he should be allowed to go everywhere. Your dad's right, though. Violet doesn't need quite that many witnesses to the birth of her baby."

Sunny noticed the data sheet on the barn wall and went to check it. Scotty had been thorough, making notations twice a day. The mare was 327 days into gestation, and everything appeared normal. Mother Nature would likely take it from here, but Sunny was glad that Jack had asked her to come. Even if her veterinarian skills weren't required, witnessing birth in any form was miraculous and soul stirring.

"I checked the foal's position," Scotty said. "Her water broke about ten minutes ago, but…"

The mare began snoring.

"Well, if that ain't the dangedest thing I've ever seen," the cowboy said, scratching his red hair.

Jack's brows raised. Apparently at a loss, he glanced from the horse to Sunny. "She's asleep?"

"Looks that way."

"Shouldn't you wake her up?"

"Let's wait a few minutes and see what happens. You say this is her first time in foal?"

"Yes."

"Likely she doesn't fully realize what's happening. We don't want to startle her."

The foal was moving inside the mare's womb, causing automatic contractions. Sunny could see the foal's front feet covered in the white birth sac, yet Violet slept on.

"You sure somebody didn't slip a tranquillizer in her feed?" Sunny asked wryly. It was pretty much a rhetorical question, but Scotty answered, anyway.

"No, ma'am. I've watched over Violet myself. When I got here this evening, though, she was straining pretty good."

"Wore herself out," Sunny commented.

Jack knelt by her side. They both had on sterile gloves in case something went wrong and they had to pull the foal. Tori and Scotty stood a few yards away, where they could see what was happening.

"Looks like this little one's determined to come into the world despite her mama's disinterest." She gave a slight tug on the foal's legs, exerting just enough pressure to get the contractions going again. "That's the way," she crooned when the muzzle showed. Quickly, she stripped away the amnion and cleared the foal's nostrils so it could breathe unimpeded, then moved back out of the way as the foal came almost completely out. Just the hind legs remained inside the mare.

Jack checked his watch. "Do we wake her up if she sleeps much longer?"

"Let's give her a few more minutes." Sunny glanced at Tori. "You doing okay, sweetie?" she asked quietly.

The girl nodded and whispered, "How come you don't take the baby all the way out?"

"See how wet she is? Violet might not understand about having a baby since she's never been through this before, but she recognizes smells. We don't want to intrude too much and have her reject her baby.''

The foal moved and brushed against Violet's leg. As though checking to see what pesky varmint was tickling her knee, Violet awoke and craned her neck around, coming face-to-face with her baby.

Unconsciously, Sunny reached over and grabbed Jack's arm, holding her breath.

After a moment of surprise, Violet licked the foal.

Sunny let out a relieved breath and carefully moved forward, crooning to the horse. As though they'd worked together as a team for years, Jack mirrored her movements. He seemed to sense what she needed and when.

He eased his hands under hers and helped her support the foal's tummy as the mare stood, breaking the umbilical cord. Sunny tied off the cord and reached for a syringe, then quickly gave the foal a tetanus shot.

''Let's back up now and let them get to know each other.''

Jack stripped off his gloves and put his hand under her elbow to help her to her feet. The front of her clothes were a mess, and she probably smelled even worse.

''So much for that scented, soothing bath,'' she said, sitting with him in the corner of the barn as the mother and baby bonded.

He leaned over, sniffed at her hair. ''You still smell like pumpkin-pie spices.''

''I didn't wash my hair. How can it smell good?''

''Don't know, but it does. Cinnamon. You wore that same scent to the prom.''

Well, there go the rules. After his strange mood this evening, she'd thought they weren't going to bring up the past. Or perhaps that had just been her admonition to herself. Still, if he viewed her as a complication, he should exercise a little more control.

"What's a prom?" Tori asked.

"A high-school dance," Jack said.

"You went to a dance with Sunny? Did you know her in the old days?"

"Ouch. Leave it to my daughter to make me feel ancient."

Tori's eyes took on a stricken look, as though she'd said something wrong. Jack hugged her to his side. "Yes. Sunny and I went to school together."

"Before you knew Mom?"

The minute she asked the question, Tori seemed to regret it. Sunny couldn't tell what the little girl was thinking. Regardless of how she felt about Lanette, for Tori, losing her mother would be devastating. Sunny might get annoyed with her own mother, but she couldn't bear the thought of never seeing her again—or feeling as though she couldn't talk about her.

"I knew your mom, too," she said, "even though she was a couple of grades ahead of me, same as your dad. And your mom worked at Wanda's Diner in town. She made pretty good malts."

Tori had withdrawn slightly and Sunny decided to change the subject. "Look. Violet's cleaning her baby. She's going to be a good mommy. In a bit, when they've bonded real good, we'll go over and you can love on the baby and let her get to know you, too, since she'll be your horse."

"It looks like her legs are gonna break," Tori said, excitement returning at the prospect of touching the little horse.

Sunny chuckled. "She'll get the hang of standing. It's instinctive."

Violet decided she'd been maternal enough for the moment and lay back down. Moments later she was snoring again. Craziest horse Sunny had ever seen.

She held out her hand for Tori. "Come on. Let's go get acquainted with that baby." The wobbly foal was sucking air and the barn wall and anything else she could get her muzzle on. They would have to get her nursing soon.

"Go ahead and hug her," Sunny said. "Pet her and rub her all over. It'll make the future veterinarian's job much easier, get her used to being poked and prodded."

Tori put her arms around the foal. They were nearly the same height. As she laid her cheek against the little horse's neck and gave it a kiss, the utter love that brightened her face was priceless.

"I can't believe she's all mine," she murmured. "She's beautiful. Can I name her Beauty?"

"You can name her anything you want," Jack said, watching his daughter with a pride only a father could display.

"This is just like having a sister." She rubbed the foal's nose and held on tight when Sunny lifted Beauty's foot to check the hoof. "How come you don't have any kids, Sunny?"

Sunny felt something twist in her stomach. "I'm not married."

"Do you want kids?"

She glanced at Jack, thought once more that this sweet child could have been their daughter.

He'd been her only boyfriend. As a teenager, aside

from her love of animals and her goal to one day work as a vet, her major focus had been marriage.

That was what she'd wanted most. Perhaps that was why she'd stuck it out so long with Michael, even when she'd realized that something was wrong.

She was approaching thirty, and her biological clock was ticking.

"Yes," she said quietly, busying herself by thumping on the bottom of Beauty's foot. "I want very much to have a family."

"Will you be Beauty's veterinarian?"

The switch in subject took her by surprise. She released the foal's leg and stood. "Only for a little while, sweetie. I have to go back to California in a few weeks." Why did saying that in front of Jack make her feel weird?

"Who's going to take care of her? Doc Levin used to come out and check Violet, but he's gone now." Tori continued to pet and stroke her new horse.

"I'm sure someone in town will hire a new vet. Don't worry, okay? Beauty looks perfectly healthy, and Violet does, too. I'll give them both a thorough examination a little later. And your dad's no slouch when it comes to taking care of animals."

"But he's not a doctor like you. I don't want to lose Beauty."

Why was she so focused on losing the foal? Then it dawned on Sunny. This child had lost her mother. And she'd obviously heard talk about the dead cattle, the reason Sunny was here. Tori was only nine years old—entirely too young to be worrying about loss.

Jack went up to his daughter, placed one hand gently on the foal and the other on Tori's cheek. "You won't lose Beauty, darlin'. She's healthy and she'll be fine. Just like I always take care of you, I can take care of Beauty, too.'' He glanced over at Sunny. ''We'll all be fine—with or without a vet.''

Sunny's heart galloped. Why had he gazed at her so intently as he'd said the words? And what in the world did he mean? His expression hadn't given anything away.

At one time, she'd been able to read Jackson Slade like a book.

Now he was an enigma. And that made her as nervous as a frog in a frying pan.

He was too potent for her peace of mind. That kiss by the back door had brought that home to her in a hurry, caused her serious concern.

Her reaction to Jack made her realize that she could easily fall for him again—for all the wrong reasons. Reasons that had to do with sex and hormones and dreams of Prince Charming.

Because despite the fact that she was a mature career woman on the verge of thirty, deep down she *was* looking for her prince.

Jack had been her fairy tale once, but he'd let her down. She'd be a fool to take a chance again.

Their lives were different now. Her foundation and her livelihood were in California. They'd gone in separate directions. No sense building castles in the air.

Chapter Eight

Sunny wiped her forehead with her sleeve, her ears ringing from the constant bawling of agitated cattle. It was late afternoon and her energy was seriously flagging, due in part from spending half the night with Tori's mare and foal.

Rain drummed down on the tin roof of the barn. The smells of wet cowhide and steamy damp earth hung heavy in the cavernous outbuilding. She flexed fingers that were stiff and forming calluses from drawing blood and giving injections.

The men had done a great job herding the cattle through the chute, working as a team so the process went smoothly and quickly. One after another, the black Angus bumped, lumbered or charged down the railed runway that cut through the barn. At the end of the passage they burst free. Junior worked the head gate, slamming it down at exactly the right instant to keep the cow from bolting out the other end of the barn, immobilizing the animal in the process.

The times he missed, everyone went into a scuffle, because by then the cow was usually good and mad.

"Only two more to go for today," Jack said, leaning close so she could hear him. He rested his hand on her shoulder and gave it a squeeze.

He, too, had stayed up late last night, but he didn't look any worse for it, darn his hide.

"I didn't realize how big your herd is."

"We'll get to the last of them by tomorrow."

And then they'd wait on tenterhooks for the lab results. Results that would either put their minds at rest or force her to start on a course that had the potential to ruin Jack.

"Okay. I'm up for two more. Bring 'em on before that thunderstorm moves over us." Relieved that the end of her day was in sight, she reached for another syringe.

The next thing she knew, she was sprawled on the other side of the barn and her right thigh was on fire with pain. Tears stung her eyes and noise roared in her head.

It took a moment for the world to come back into focus. *Holy crud.*

Jack was shouting orders over the bawling of the two remaining steers. Junior, Lou, Duane and Scotty muscled them back into the shute.

Within seconds, Jack was at Sunny's side, kneeling next to her. "Are you okay? Can you catch your breath? Where did she get you?"

"Hold on a minute," Sunny said. His eyes and hands seemed to be touching her everywhere. She was dazed enough by the cow's unexpected kick; Jack's nearness and attentiveness weren't helping to clear her head. "I'm fine."

"Your face is as white as a bleached sheet."

"I just need a minute. This isn't the first time I've been laid out by a nervous cow."

"I should have been paying better attention. I was right beside you."

"It wasn't your fault, Jack. That's the thing about cattle. They don't bother to warn you when they're going to cut loose. They'll stand there chewing their cud, happy as you please, not a single flick of an ear or bat of their eye. Then whammo, you're picking your broken body up out of the hay." She was still squeezing her leg, could feel the stickiness of blood through the denim.

"Do you think something's broken?"

"Doubt it." *Maybe.* She started to get up.

Jack put a hand on her shoulder and gently pushed her back down. "Why are you holding your leg like that? Let me see."

"It's nothing."

"I'll be the judge." He pried her hand off her thigh, his brows drawing together when he saw the tear in her jeans where the hoof had caught her. "That doesn't look like nothing to me. You're bleeding pretty hard."

"It's just a scratch, Jack. No big deal. Now, move out of my way and let me up. I've got only two more cows to go."

"*I've* only got two more cows to go. *You're* going to stay put."

Her temper flashed at Jack's bossing her around. That he was clearly concerned about her faded to the background. "In case you've forgotten, this is my profession and I'm perfectly capable of—"

He pointed a finger at her and stood. "Don't move. And I mean it, Sunny. After 938 cows, I think I've got the hang of what we're doing." He whirled around and grabbed a clean syringe out of her kit.

A tense moment passed, then Sunny relaxed back against the wall. Or tried to, at least. Her leg was burning and aching clear to the bone. If she wasn't looking at it with her own eyes, she'd seriously wonder whether it was still attached.

The last annoyed Angus was released from the ranch hands' headlock and shooed out of the barn. Jack sealed the specimens he'd collected, instructed Scotty to get this batch to town and send it overnight to California, then peeled off his gloves and walked toward Sunny. She had to admit she was glad the day was over.

She put her hands by her hips to boost herself up off the ground, but Jack stopped her.

"Hang on." He leaned down and scooped her up in his arms as though she weighed little more than a feed sack.

"Oh, for...you don't have to—damn it, I can walk."

"We don't know that yet. And I'd just as soon be in the house if you put weight on this leg and pass out on me."

"I've never passed out in my life."

"There's always a first time."

Feeling ridiculous, Sunny glanced around and noticed that the men were watching. Indignant, she said, "I hope you know you're causing a scene over nothing. Would you carry another vet like this?"

"Hell, no. Doc Levin is ugly as sin and weighs a good two hundred fifty pounds. Grab our hats."

"What?"

"The hats, sugar bear. It's raining, and my hands are full."

"Well, if you'd put me down like I asked they

wouldn't be full.'' When he neared the peg by the barn door, she snatched down both their hats, plopped hers on her head and shoved his Stetson on his.

''A little lower, okay?''

She huffed out a breath and tugged the brim lower on his forehead.

She knew he was trying not to jostle her as he walked, but her leg throbbed nonetheless. The rain had tapered off to a sprinkle, but an angry-looking thunderhead loomed above them, blocking the sun and turning the air to thick steam. The sky was going to open up any minute now.

He went around to the front door—which she thought was odd—and scraped his muddy boots on the porcupine mat.

''No sense in getting Beau in a dither,'' he said as though reading her mind. ''He can be worse than an old maid.''

When he pushed open the door and kicked it shut with his foot, Simba raised his head from where he and Tori were playing on the landing at the top of the stairs. The dog leaped to his feet and bounded down the steps three at a time. He barked once, then stretched his neck, licking where he could reach.

''I'm okay, boy.''

Simba wasn't buying it, and Jack swore softly as he nearly tripped over the anxious dog accompanying them back up the steps.

Tori hadn't moved an inch. Her eyes were wide and stunned.

''Jack,'' Sunny whispered. ''Put me down.''

''In a minute.''

''We're scaring Tori.''

He glanced at his daughter and kept moving. ''Tori,

darlin', would you take care of Simba for a few minutes more? Sunny got kicked by one of the cows, and we just need to put a bandage on her leg, okay?''

Tori nodded and caught Simba around the neck, curling her fingers in his fur. After sitting back down, she drew the dog close. "Cora went home. Do you want me to get Beau?''

"We'll be fine. Maybe you could ask Beau to make Sunny some tea.''

Tori popped up, obviously relieved to have a job to do.

"With lots of sugar,'' Sunny called.

Jack took her into the master bathroom, where he carefully lowered her onto the closed lid of the toilet.

"Well, that's amazing,'' she commented. "A man who puts the lid down.''

"The cat has a weird toilet fetish. She likes to get in it.'' He plucked Sunny's hat off, then his own, and set them both on the sink counter.

"Guess nobody ever told her cats don't like water,'' she stated wryly.

"Guess not. Think you can put weight on the leg?''

"Of course.'' Her words were much braver than she felt. She gripped the edge of the sink to pull herself up, dreading the movement. Perspiration beaded on her brow, dripped between her breasts. The denim was sticking to the wound, and bending her leg caused her skin to tug.

She hated showing weakness, had no patience with it.

"Not so fast,'' Jack said, gently holding her arms. He helped her to stand, steadied her as she tested her weight on the leg.

It held fine. "I told you it wasn't broken.'' To prove

it, she took a few tentative steps across the bathroom, Jack hovering over her every inch of the way. "I'm sure it's just bruised."

"Well, you've got fresh blood coming out now. Let's have a look and see if you're going to need stitches."

"I'll take care of it."

He just stood there stubbornly.

Sunny had trouble holding strong against his stare. "In order to get at it, I have to take off my pants."

His eyebrows rose. "It's not as though I haven't seen a female body in underwear."

Yes, he'd seen *hers*.

"You are wearing underwear, aren't you?"

"Of course." *Sort of.*

"Then what's the problem?" He reached for the snap of her jeans. She batted his hands away.

"Listen, Sunny. I'm not leaving this bathroom until I've checked that wound and cleaned it. Either that or I'm hauling you into town to the doctor."

"I don't need a doctor."

"Then stop being a sissy and let's do this."

Even though she flushed from head to toe, she jerked the zipper down and gingerly tugged her jeans to her knees.

The man still knew how to rile her.

She was *not* a sissy.

Bent over, she got a look at the gash. A hoof-size circle of raw skin surrounded a deeper laceration on her thigh, but it didn't appear to require a stitch. Still, the action of pulling rough denim over the wound made her head spin and nausea churn her stomach.

Jack wrapped his hands around Sunny's hips to

steady her, trying not to notice or react to the cotton thong that left her behind exposed.

"Sit."

"I do believe I will."

Pale as all get-out and she could still sass, make light of an incident that would have traumatized most women and had them screaming for drugs. He guided her back down on the toilet, and gathered a washcloth and first-aid kit from beneath the sink.

The image of her sailing through the barn and crumpling in a heap in the corner was etched in his mind, playing over and over like a disaster video clip on the six o'clock news. In the seconds it had taken him to get to her, he'd thought his heart would stop.

Seeing the broken, swollen skin up close made his gut churn anew. "See, you're not invincible after all."

"I never said I was."

"Actions speak louder than words."

"What—ouch!" She tried to push his hand away when he washed the cut.

"Don't be a baby." He wanted to kiss the wound and make it better. He hated like hell that he was hurting her, hated that she'd gotten hurt in the first place.

"You're hardly bigger than a minute, yet without an ounce of hesitation you wade right into the midst of animals that could probably flatten you with a flick of their tail."

"Training surpasses stature—" She sucked in a breath. "Damn it, do you have to rub so hard?"

"There's dirt embedded in your skin, Sunny. When's the last time you had a tetanus shot?"

"Last year."

He looked up. "What happened?"

She held up her palm, indicating the scar there.

"Rusty nail in a fence post." He could tell she wanted to add "So there!" and his lips twitched.

"So, you don't spend *all* your time in a lab?" He poured peroxide on the wound and blew on it to ease the sting.

"Um…"

He glanced up. She was watching him blow on her thigh, her full lips slightly parted, her green eyes transfixed in a sort of dazed sensuality.

His gut tightened, and so did the rest of his body. Every so often, in unguarded moments, he saw glimpses of the old Sunny, the girl he'd once known. The girl who'd turned him inside out and held his heart in her hand.

She could turn him on with just a glance.

He knew he'd played a big part in erecting the wall she hid behind most of the time. He'd done something incredibly stupid. He knew that, took full responsibility for his actions.

But Sunny hadn't been blameless, either.

And when she'd walked out on him, she'd left a cavern-size hole in his soul.

"The lab?" he prodded, blotting her wound with a tissue.

"Oh. I've done mostly in-house research and study this past year. But I still like to get out and investigate livestock firsthand when I can."

"That's not really in your job description anymore, though?"

"Technically, no. We have a team of vets who actually collect samples and do the hands-on work."

"Do you like what you do?" He dabbed antibacterial salve on the raw skin and covered it with a gauze pad.

"I care about keeping animals healthy."

"That's not what I asked." He took a stretchy wrap-type bandage and wound it completely around her thigh to hold the gauze in place.

"Yes, I like what I do." Her tone was exasperated. Before he could complete a second loop with the bandage, she put her hand over his. "Isn't this a bit of overkill? All I need are a couple pieces of tape, not a leg cast. Besides, I'm going to take a shower, and all your hard work is just going to get wet and have to be redone."

He unwound the elastic material and set the supplies on the sink, then reached for the heel of her boot.

"Now what—"

"You said you wanted a shower. I don't imagine those jeans are going to come off over the boots. Unless you had in mind to shower with your pants on?" He peeled off her boots and socks and tugged her jeans the rest of the way off. She sat there in her long-sleeved shirt and white cotton thong.

It'd be best all around if he got out of this bathroom before he did something else incredibly stupid—like run his hands over every inch of her skin, satisfying himself with the remembered feel of her sexy body. Physical work kept her muscles toned and shapely. He imagined his palm could probably span her hipbones and cup her behind at the same time.

He got up and twisted the hot-water faucet in the shower, his nerves and his libido screaming. "Let me know when you're done and I'll finish the bandage."

She stood, and the hem of her shirt fell to her thighs, preserving her modesty, shielding that little bitty panty from view. The sight was almost more erotic than if she'd been totally naked.

"I can take care of it myself."

He shrugged, plucked his hat off the counter and let himself out of the bathroom.

Her answer about liking her job hadn't rung true. The woman he'd known ten years ago wouldn't have been satisfied cooped up indoors. The woman he'd seen cooing and cussing at his cattle these past two days definitely belonged in the field.

Animals were her passion.

That she'd traded her passion for watching rats run around in mazes, and had delegated the field work to others, was a crying shame.

THE SPRAY STUNG LIKE FIRE against her leg, so Sunny didn't linger under the water. Besides, she'd had to use Jack's soap and shampoo instead of her own, since he'd practically pushed her into his shower. Her cosmetics were in the guest bathroom.

The spicy scent—the scent of Jack—was wreaking havoc on her system.

She shut off the water, twisted one towel over her hair and another around herself and contemplated what to do now. She'd have to streak through his room and down the hall to get to her bedroom. And she wouldn't put it past him to be waiting for her, ready to inspect her first-aid job.

After dabbing more salve on the wound, she rummaged around in the medical supplies until she located a large, square bandage. She pulled the tapes off the ends, fitted the bandage over the open cut and gave it a pat. The way Jack had tried to truss her up, a person would think she'd nearly had her leg cut off instead of having received a harmless scrape.

She had to admit, though, that the "harmless

scrape'' hurt like the dickens. Once she'd grabbed up her dirty clothes, she peeked out the door. Seeing the coast was clear, she sprinted across the room and down the hall, nearly tripping over Simba as he pushed in ahead of her.

''I thought you'd dumped me for Tori,'' she said to the dog.

Simba licked her knee, and she reached down to pat his head. ''I'm kidding. It's sweet of you to keep her company. She's a normal little girl, but there's a reserve about her that worries me.'' Simba cocked his ears, and Sunny patted him again. ''If anybody can get her to loosen up, it'll be you, big guy. Who can resist you?''

Her cell phone rang in the pocket of the jeans she still held, and she jumped like a scalded cat. Without checking the caller ID, she answered.

''Did you wrap your leg?''

For a minute, she was confused. ''Jack? Where are you?''

''Downstairs.''

Okay, now she was hallucinating. ''Why are you calling me on the phone?''

''To make sure you followed instructions. Did you want me to come up there and check?''

She leaned against the closed door, clutching the towel as though he could see through the phone that she was half-naked.

Beneath his moodiness, Jack had a compassionate streak as wide as Texas. It was sweet. And it made her feel special. Michael wouldn't have even noticed that she'd hurt herself, much less insisted on doctoring her.

''I'm a big girl,'' she said softly.

"And stubborn," he countered.

"A trait we obviously still share." Talking on the phone when they were both in the same house seemed...intimate, illicit.

"You've got a bad habit of not answering direct questions, sugar."

"Oh, don't fuss. I know how to put on a bandage."

"Did you wrap it the way I showed you?"

"Jack?"

"What?"

"I'm hanging up now." She pressed the button and smiled. Fatherhood had evidently turned him into a worrier.

An odd thought struck her. How had he known her cell phone number?

Before she could lower the phone, it rang again. She shook her head and grinned, ready for him this time. "You are such a pervert. You just want another look at my thong."

"Oh...are you getting crank calls, dear?"

"Mama?" *Holy crud!* "Um...no, I was—I thought you were Donetta. Sorry."

Liar, liar, pants on fire.

"No wonder there was no answer the first time I tried. That girl does love her shoes, though she should have better support than flimsy thongs since she's on her feet all day. If she's asking to borrow yours, tell her no. Her podiatrist will thank you."

Shoes? Sunny nearly laughed. For once she was happy that her mother had jumped to the wrong conclusion.

"What's up?"

"I fixed supper and overcalculated. You know how I am when I get in the kitchen. I made enough to feed half the county. And I can't have it going to waste. Since you and Jack are over there, working your fingers to the bone, I thought you'd appreciate a nice home-cooked meal.''

"Mama..." Sunny deliberately put a warning note in her voice. "What are you up to?" Matchmaking was her guess.

"What's wrong with inviting my own daughter to supper?"

"I'm sure Beau has already started to cook—"

"Oh, no. I checked with Cora and told her I was planning dinner. And Jack said he'd be happy to come."

Sunny frowned. "He did? When?"

"When I phoned the ranch a few minutes ago. He agreed, but he suggested I phone you, as well."

Aha. "Did you, by chance, give him my cell number?"

"I didn't think you would mind. I'm sure you've been quite busy, and those details do tend to slip our minds. Anyway, I'll expect you all at seven. That's what time I told the others."

"What others?"

"Just Storm and your girlfriends."

Sunny sighed. Her leg was starting to throb again. She'd hoped for a nice relaxing night, some pain meds, a good book and the sound of rain tapping at the windows.

She wished her mother had asked her first before going ahead with the plans. But Mama liked to get her own way.

Still... "Mama, you brought me back to Texas to do a job."

"You can't work both day and night, honey. Besides, I've made fried chicken with milk gravy, just the way you like it.''

"Oh, you're sneaky.'' Fatigue and pain didn't have a prayer of standing up against Anna Carmichael's cooking. "Did you do up a cheesecake?''

"With lemon custard on top. And a peanut-butter cream pie for Jack and Tori. Cora tells me that's their favorite.''

"It's Simba's, too.''

Anna gave a long-suffering sigh. "I'll cut the silly dog a sliver, and not a bite more. Honestly, Sunny Leigh, you're a veterinarian. You ought to know better than to feed your dog sweets.''

Of course she did. "That's a problem when the dog doesn't think he's a dog.''

"Well, he's not sitting at my dining-room table and that's that. See you at seven?''

"Seven's good.'' She hung up the phone and glanced at Simba. "Grandma made peanut-butter pie.'' Simba thumped his tail against the wood floor. "No sitting on the dining-room chairs, though. She'll lose every bit of her good humor.''

SUNNY DRESSED IN A PAIR of loose, silky cabana pants that tied at the waist just below her navel, a white tank top and a pair of sandals. The red-and-white Hawaiian print on the pants might look out of place on a cattle ranch, but the fabric was the most forgiving against her sore leg. It didn't cling or rub.

When she came down the stairs, Jack and Tori were waiting for her. His gaze drank her in as though she was a potent, fruity cocktail and he was dying to take a sip.

The hunger in his eyes made her heart trip. He was

the kind of man who made a woman forget her own mind. Snug jeans and a crisp white T-shirt tucked into the waistband complemented his excellent physique. The diamond earring winking in his ear and the too-long hair gave him the look of a rebel.

The contrast of his daughter's small hand in his large masculine one made Sunny's heart melt, even as a sharp pain lanced her chest. Although she adored Victoria, the hurt over Jack's marrying another woman was still alive inside her. She'd been so sure she'd dealt with it years ago.

"Ready?" he asked.

She nodded and went down the rest of the stairs.

Jack reached for her elbow. "You're limping. Are you sure you're up to this?"

"Knowing my mother, how can you even ask such a question? Mama doesn't invite—she commands."

"I can call and cancel," he said softly. "She'd understand."

Yes, her mother would accept the cancellation if it came from Jack. But Sunny still had a full day of work ahead of her tomorrow on the ranch, and if she ducked out on dinner, it would create the wrong impression. And Jack would hover the way he had this afternoon. She'd been kicked and stomped on before and never missed a day of work.

She stepped out of his gentle hold. "Are you kidding? No skittish cow's gonna make me miss fried chicken and lemon-custard cheesecake. Besides, she's also invited Donetta, Tracy and Becca. Storm, too, so you won't be the only rooster in a barnful of hens."

He shrugged and reached for his hat, then tucked it low on his forehead. "I can hold my own among a bunch of females."

"I'll just bet you can."

The barest hint of a smile tipped his lips, and his blue eyes twinkled with enough seductive wattage to light the town. Needing to put a little space between her and Jack, she reached for Tori's hand. "Come on, sugar. Let's you and me hobble to the car."

He muttered something that sounded suspiciously like "chicken." She didn't think he was referring to supper, but she ignored him.

He'd had his hands on her entirely too much for one day.

Chapter Nine

Tori held tight to Sunny as they walked to the car. The little girl was as bad as her father, watching over Sunny in case she made a misstep and hurt herself again.

The rain had stopped, but the ground was still damp, so the soles of Sunny's sandals were slick.

"Beau said he saw somebody get kicked by a cow once and it knocked the man clean out the barn door. Did that happen to you, Sunny?"

"No, sugar. I stayed inside the barn." *Barely.* She reached into her purse and rummaged around.

"Leave your keys right where they are," Jack said from behind her. "You're not driving."

Instead of glaring back at him, she continued to feel for her keys. "Does he boss you like this?" she asked Tori.

The child darted a glance at her dad. "No. I'm a pretty good girl," she said softly.

How odd, Sunny thought. One minute Tori had been fishing for gory details, and the next she'd gone as quiet and polite as a church maiden.

"Well, I've always been a little on the wild side. Must be why he gets bossy with me." She finally found her keys. Digging in an oversize bag with one hand and holding Tori's in the other was difficult.

She turned toward the Suburban, but Jack slung his arm around her shoulders and steered her in the opposite direction with hardly any effort at all.

"I'm bigger than you are," he said.

She dropped her keys back into her bag. No sense arguing. "I'm operating under a handicap, or you'd never get away with that."

He glanced down at her leg.

"Not that handicap," she said. "I make it a point not to brawl in front of children."

He shot her a grin, and the power of it sent a punch of excitement right through her stomach.

"You and me brawling? Now, that sounds interesting. Can I have a rain check?" When he opened the back door of the truck's crew cab, Simba leaped off the porch steps and ran flat-out to bound into the back seat.

Jack swore as the dog left muddy paw prints nearly the size of a bear's on his floor mats and upholstery.

"Simba's invited to dinner, too," Sunny said, trying hard to contain her smile. "See what happens when you push to get your way without gathering all the facts?"

"Why can't he ride in the bed like any other civilized dog?"

"He's a little clumsy at times. Has trouble staying on his feet in a moving vehicle. Being back there tends to make him carsick. That's not a pretty sight."

"Is he going to get sick in my truck?"

"Oh, no. Not as long as he rides inside and can see out the window." Jack was looking at her as though she'd just landed from another planet. She shrugged.

"You and my mother can commiserate. She's not crazy about him sitting on her dining-room chairs."

Jack opened his mouth as if to speak, then shut it and shook his head. He was about to hoist Tori into the truck when Duane Keegan walked up.

"Just thought I'd let you know we got those boards replaced in the barn."

"Good. Is the herd settled?"

"Like lambs." Duane looked over at Sunny. "How's the leg?"

"It'll be fine by tomorrow."

"You shook us up for a minute there." He gazed down at Tori and smiled, then crouched and touched a finger to her cheek. "Hey, pretty girl."

Tori shrank back against Jack's leg as though she wanted to make herself invisible. "Hello," she said politely.

After an awkward moment, Duane stood, shifted on his feet. Sunny knew he'd been trying to be friendly, and could tell that Tori was uneasy. It was odd. Duane was one of the nicest, most easygoing guys on the ranch, always willing to help out.

Yet she'd noticed that the only men Tori seemed to be comfortable with were Jack and Beau. Tori had built a shell around herself. Sunny recognized the signs because she'd built one of her own.

Shells caused loneliness, even though they protected a person from hurt. But a nine-year-old shouldn't be lonely. She shouldn't be so willing to please, so focused on being good.

Stepping between Duane and Tori, Sunny hoisted the little girl up into the back seat. "Let's hop in the truck while your daddy talks business."

Simba quivered all over at having company, and

gave Tori a quick lick on her cheek. The child giggled and Sunny relaxed. That was more like it.

While she was here, maybe she could find out what weighed so heavily on Tori's small shoulders. Jack was an excellent father, openly displaying his love for his daughter, so that wasn't the problem.

Perhaps a woman's touch was needed. Little girls were supposed to be spontaneous, have fun, throw fits, speak without censoring themselves.

Bringing Tori Slade out of her shyness would be a perfect project for the Texas Sweethearts, Sunny decided. She'd have to get her pals off to the side to decide on a strategy, though. All four of them were stubborn and outspoken, which could, on occasion, cause the fur to fly.

Sunny mentally rubbed her hands together. Helping Tori was a good plan. Worthwhile.

And it would give her another goal to work toward while she was here, occupy her mind so Jack wouldn't take up so much space in her thoughts.

THE MINUTE THEY WALKED in the door of the colonial-style ranch house, Anna hovered, her sharp eyes not missing a trick. "Sunny, are you limping?"

"I don't think so." She'd tried her best to walk normally. That Simba had jumped in her lap right before she'd gotten out of the truck hadn't helped.

"Yes, you are. What did you do to yourself?"

Sunny sighed, knew she'd better fess up. Otherwise they'd be standing in the entry hall all night. "Just a little accident with one of the cows. It's nothing."

"Nothing, my foot. I talked to you on the phone. You didn't say a word about an accident. Let me see."

"Mama, I'm not dropping my pants so you can look at my leg."

Jack raised a brow as if to say she was on her own and he didn't mind watching the show.

"Did I hear someone was stripping out here?" Storm asked, coming into the front room.

"No one's stripping."

"Sunny's hurt," Anna announced, hands on her hips.

"I'm not hurt. Darn it, Jack. Don't just stand there. Back me up before she calls the paramedics."

He actually had the nerve to pat her on the shoulder, as though he feared she was on the verge of hysteria and needed placating.

"The hoof caught her pretty good, Mrs. C., but I cleaned the wound myself."

That effectively hushed Anna. She looked at him the way she did most males—with absolute reverence and respect. "Well then. I'm sure you did an excellent job. I know my daughter's in good hands with you, Jack."

He preened and Sunny nearly gagged. Her mother was a champion when it came to catering to men and their egos. She did it in a motherly, perfectly Southern way.

Before they could move out of the front hall, another car pulled into the driveway. Tracy Lynn was driving her flashy convertible Mustang, with the top down. Donetta, riding shotgun, held a scarf over her hair, and Becca Sue had the back seat to herself. The radio was cranked up so high that folks a mile away could enjoy it whether they wanted to or not.

Doing a fairly good impression of Mario Andretti, Tracy Lynn wheeled the sporty car beneath the portico as her passengers grabbed for a solid surface to brace themselves. Shania Twain's voice stopped in mid syllable when the engine shut off.

"Pretty gutsy," Jack commented. "I suppose your sweethearts don't realize it's been raining all day."

Sunny immediately jumped to her friends' defense. "The storm's already moved on. And it's plenty warm out to ride with the top down."

"Steamy, you mean. The mosquitoes will eat them for supper."

Sunny laughed. "You think a mosquito could keep up with her driving?"

"You're right."

Tracy took a moment to raise the convertible top in case of another unexpected shower, then the women filed in, passing out hugs and kisses all around.

"I ought to cite you for violating the county's excessive noise ordinance with that music," Storm said to Tracy Lynn as he bent for a hug.

"You wouldn't dare," she replied with a flirtatious laugh. "Besides, my daddy'd just fix it for me."

"Don't bet on it," Storm told her, his lips twitching. "The mayor and I have a professional understanding."

Donetta whipped off her scarf and fluffed her riot of red curls; her matching red brows arched. "Hmm... I wonder how far professional understanding would stretch if Mayor Randolph found out how our esteemed sheriff built himself a nice little moonshine business right in the attic of his mother's house."

"Storm Carmichael," Anna said. "You did not!"

"See?" Storm said with a smirk. "My mom begs to differ." He grinned and kissed Becca's cheek, then snagged Donetta around the waist as she attempted to sashay by him, and drew her into a playful hug. With her trendy platform shoes adding a good four inches to her already impressive five-foot-ten, she was nearly as tall as he was.

If Sunny hadn't been watching, she'd have missed the slight stiffening when Donetta's body came into contact with Storm's. They'd all grown up together, and physical displays of affection came naturally.

So what in the world had that blip been all about?

She met her brother's gaze and he merely winked at her. Then Anna was ushering everyone into the dining room, fussing at Simba with every step as the dog kept dancing around her, tripping her as she rushed around setting heaping platters of food on the table.

"Simba," Sunny called. "Remember what I told you."

Simba charged back to Sunny's side like a perfect gentleman.

"What did you tell him?" Tori asked.

"Just that he had to behave, and that if he wants dessert he can't sit on a dining-room chair."

Tori smiled, a dimple creasing her cheek. "Does he like to sit on chairs?"

"All the time. He's been extra good at your house, though. I think Beau scares him."

"Does your mom really let him have dessert?"

Sunny leaned down and cupped her hand to Tori's ear. "It's really a doggie treat," she whispered, "but he thinks it's peanut-butter pie."

Tori nodded and whispered back, "Okay, I won't tell him."

"I knew I could count on you. We'll have to make you an honorary Texas Sweetheart." She saw Simba eyeing her mother's ceramic rooster and darted over to grab his collar just in time. ''You can't lick the rooster, Simba. We discussed that, remember? You nearly knocked it off the sideboard the other day. Now, lie down and be a good boy. I'll let you know when it's time for dessert.''

Simba obediently lay down and put his nose on his paws. He stuck his tongue out a couple of times, as though he could already taste his promised treat.

When Sunny straightened, she nearly collided with Jack.

''What isn't my daughter going to tell me?''

He was so close she could feel his belt buckle pressing against her side. Figuring out what the heck he was talking about took her a minute. Then she realized he'd heard Tori's promise not to tell.

She gave him a look of pure innocence. ''Why in the world would you assume we were talking about you?''

''You said 'him.'''

''You're not the only 'him' in this herd, cowboy.'' Stepping away from him, she put her hands on Tori's slim shoulders and maneuvered her around the table. ''You sit by me, sugar.''

Sunny slid into the empty chair next to her mother's place at the head of the table and sat Tori between herself and Becca, leaving Jack to fend for himself at the other end.

Good. She wanted plenty of space separating them. The feel of his warm breath on her neck as he'd tried to get her to confess she'd been talking about him had made her shiver. She couldn't deny that he aroused her—he was an attractive man.

But she wasn't about to raise speculations among

her family and friends when she had no intention of taking up with Jack again.

"What's a Texas Sweetheart?" Tori asked, politely placing her napkin in her lap.

"It's a group for girls only. Becca, Tracy, Donetta and I started it when we were about your age. When you're a Texas Sweetheart, it means you're best friends forever, no matter what. You get to tell your secrets and nobody will breathe a word of it outside the circle."

"And you have to stick up for one another," Becca commented from her place next to Tori. "Just like Donetta did when Storm threatened to give Tracy Lynn a ticket."

"Exactly," Sunny said. "Even though Donetta hates the way Tracy Lynn drives, she's honor-bound to stand up for her pal."

"What's wrong with my driving?" Tracy asked. She and Donetta were sitting directly across the table from Sunny, Tori and Becca, segregating Jack and Storm at the opposite end.

"We don't have nearly enough time to go into that," Donetta said dryly. "Besides, that was my Shania Twain tape I was defending."

"And your sneaky fingers on the volume knob," Tracy added.

"There is that. However, if the ticket threat had been for speeding, I'd have probably signed the affidavit myself, corroborating the infraction, then gone straight out to hang my panties on Bertha."

Storm choked on a sip of iced tea.

Jack cleared his throat.

"Girls," Anna admonished, although there was no bite in her voice, only indulgence.

Sunny leaned toward Tori, whose eyes were agog as her gaze bounced from woman to woman. "Bertha's a big cottonwood tree out by the river. If one of the sweethearts causes a stir, hanging her underpants on a branch is the penalty."

"You wouldn't have to do that, though," Becca said. "New members get a whole year's grace period."

"I'm very good," Tori said solemnly. "I hardly ever cause a stir."

Sunny's heart squeezed. She dropped a kiss on the top of the child's head. "Then it's official. We'll have an induction ceremony next time we're at the beauty salon."

As Donetta commented on the merits of holding ceremonies at her shop, Sunny glanced at her mother. There was a speculative look in Anna's eye as she gazed from Sunny to Tori and back again.

Uh-oh.

Leaning over, Sunny whispered, "Don't get any ideas, Mama."

"Did I say anything?"

"You don't have to. You've got that look."

"I was merely going to comment on how good you are with children," she said quietly.

Well, duh, Sunny thought, exchanging glances with Donetta and Tracy. She avoided looking at Jack, though she didn't think her mother's voice had carried down the table.

Still, Mama was about as subtle as a stallion at a teasing rail when she got it in her head to matchmake. And from the pleased smile on her face, that was exactly what she was up to, already itching to boast to Trudy Fay Simon that she was finally a grandmother.

In a show of pure dramatics, Anna suddenly popped up as though she'd sat on a tack. "Goodness. We're terribly unbalanced. Jack, you come down here."

"I'm good, Mrs. C."

"Nonsense. Storm, switch sides and sit between Donetta and Tracy Lynn. They need a referee, anyway. You girls slide over," she directed Becca, Tori and Sunny.

Simba thought it was a fun game of musical chairs he ought to take part in. But before Anna's commands could be obeyed, Storm's cell phone rang.

"Sorry," he said. "I'm on call."

Sunny noticed that Jack hadn't moved from his spot, either. He was watching Storm, and he seemed to be eavesdropping on her brother's phone conversation.

That was weird.

Storm dropped his cell phone back in his pocket and looked at Jack, who nodded. Now Sunny was really curious. Since when had Jack and Storm started communicating silently?

"There's a wreck out on the main highway. A tanker truck spilled its load. Sorry about dinner, Mom."

"I'll pack you some food to go." Anna immediately went into action, used to this sort of thing. "No sense in you boys going hungry."

"I doubt we'll have time to eat," Storm said.

"Nonsense. I ordered an excellent cooler through my cooking catalog." She retrieved a collapsible, insulated container from the sideboard and began loading it with chicken and biscuits.

Sunny noticed that Tori's hands were folded tightly in her lap and that her eyes were glued to her father.

She put her arm around the little girl, confused when Jack rounded the table and crouched next to Tori's chair.

"Do you have to go, Daddy?"

"Yes, sweetheart. Remember how we talked about always keeping our promises?"

Tori nodded.

Sunny felt a jolt behind her breastbone. He hadn't kept his promise to *her*.

"Why are you going with Storm?" she asked.

His blue eyes shifted to hers and held, bringing old memories boiling to the surface.

"I'm on call, too. I'm a reserve deputy."

"Oh." She hadn't known that. She felt totally out of the loop, because no one else at the table found it odd that he was leaving. Then again, that was her fault. She'd acted ugly on occasion when anyone had tried to talk about Jack.

He focused his attention back on Tori. "We need to hurry now, sweetheart, so I can run you home to stay with Beau."

"You don't have to do that." Sunny realized that she was still stroking Tori's shoulder. "She can stay and eat with us, and I'll take her home."

"I'm not sure...." He studied his daughter's expression, the way a parent who knew how to gauge his child's moods and wants would.

"It's okay, Daddy. I know you have important work to do. I'll stay with Sunny."

The surprise that showed on his face was quickly masked. "You're sure?"

She nodded.

He kissed Tori's cheek and stood. "I'll come in and say good-night to you when I get home." He fished his keys out of his pocket and looked at Sunny. "How's your leg feel? Will you be okay driving my truck?"

"Oh, for heaven's sake. My leg's fine and I can certainly drive a vehicle. But how are you going to get home?"

"I'll hitch a ride with someone."

"We'll drive Sunny and Tori home," Tracy Lynn said.

Skepticism flashed in Jack's eyes, probably because of Donetta's comments over Tracy's driving, Sunny thought. Or maybe because the word *home* was being bandied about so freely and easily.

An odd sensation fluttered in her stomach. They were acting an awful lot like a family, coordinating who got the car, what to do with the kid and where everyone would be.

If she were eighteen again, with her dreams and future plans still wrapped up in Jack, she could imagine fast-forwarding ten years and picturing this exact scenario.

Donetta made a shooing motion with her hand. "They'll be safe, Jack. Tracy Lynn's only a terror when we egg her on."

"Donetta, you're not helping," Becca said, frowning. "Tracy Lynn's a good driver, Jack. Go on, now."

"Jack?" Storm called from the doorway. "We gotta roll."

"I'm right behind you." He kissed Tori again, started to reach out to Sunny, then dropped his hand. "Thanks for watching her for me."

"No problem. We'll have a great time."

Anna shoved containers of food at the men as they

left. "You call, now, if any of our people are involved in the wreck."

Both Storm and Jack nodded. Sunny figured that if they'd known anyone in the accident, word would have already reached them. Hope Valley's information line was faster than God's.

Tori kept her eyes on her father until she could no longer see him.

Sunny fiddled with her silverware. Lord, that had felt weird. The men going off to work, the women staying behind—and *she* was in charge of Jack's daughter.

Handing over that responsibility hadn't been easy for him. She'd seen his reluctance, his worry. He was very protective of his little girl.

And right now, his daughter was looking terribly lost.

Can't have that on my *watch,* Sunny thought.

When the front door closed behind the men, she slapped her palms on the table, causing the silverware, dishes and everyone there to jump.

"Hot dog, let's have a girl party!"

Tracy Lynn, Donetta and Becca sprang from their seats without a second's hesitation. Time and distance hadn't weakened the bonds of the Texas Sweethearts, or their ability to react as one. The immediate, laughter-filled scramble altered the atmosphere in the dining room in less time than it took to flip a light switch.

Sunny scooted her chair back and plucked Tori out of hers. "Follow me, sugar."

"Girls," Anna started to admonish, but Donetta pulled her up, as well, while Becca punched the Play button on the stereo tucked discreetly between the bookshelf and china display.

Anna had the stereo tuned to an oldies station, and a silly song about a purple people eater blared out. Tracy Lynn squealed and started a conga line.

After grabbing two chicken drumsticks off the platter, Sunny handed one to Tori and bit into the other, chewing and singing along with the song at the same time. Her leg protested, but she ignored it.

Tori didn't seem too sure about the sudden craziness. Reserved and wary, she followed Becca, with Sunny, Anna and Donetta completing the line.

Putting her hands on Tori's shoulders, Sunny gave a wiggle, encouraging the little girl to pick up the rhythm. The fried chicken leg in her hand poked against Tori's cheek. Simba darted forward, quickly lapped Tori's face and kept right on going, turning in circles and barking at the fun.

Sunny burst out laughing and Tori's own small giggle soon became a genuine belly laugh.

As they danced around the table, Anna smiled at the sight of Tori relaxing and joining in the silliness. "Oh, what the heck." She gave a chortle of delight and took a piece of chicken off the platter herself, then waved her arms in the air and swished her hips as she bobbed and sang about purple people eaters.

Donetta pitched a biscuit to Becca. Seeing grown women tossing food and dancing around the dining-room table like fools seemed to unlock something in Tori.

The little girl slipped two spoons from the table and used them as batons while she dipped, hopped and swayed behind Becca.

Sunny's heart melted. Now, *this* was how a nine-year-old should act.

Never let it be said that the Texas Sweethearts

couldn't show a person how a cow should eat his cabbage!

Too bad Jack wasn't here to see his little girl cut loose.

A part of Sunny wanted him to remember, when she was back home in California, that *she'd* accomplished this turnaround.

No sooner did that thought surface than her heart thudded and her breath lodged in her lungs, making her feel as though she was having a full-blown panic attack. She shouldn't be imagining Jack thinking about her at all.

From the moment she'd received her mother's phone call, she promised herself she would stay strong, keep her emotional distance. She'd been confident that after ten years, she could face her past and do what she had to do.

The problem was, the more tangled up she got in Jack's and Tori's lives, the more difficult it would be for her to leave.

She'd left Hope Valley once before with her heart aching, feeling as if a rug had been snatched from beneath her feet. She'd stumbled through her days in a fog and sobbed her soul dry at nights, the agony inside her never letting go.

It had nearly shattered her.

That was one of the reasons she'd stayed away so long.

At this moment, she feared it hadn't been long enough.

Chapter Ten

It was late when Jack got back from the accident scene, but Sunny was still awake. She saw the flash of his headlights outside, heard the tired scuff of his boots on the stairs, listened to the rush of water through the pipes as he showered.

Knowing that he was in the house, right across the hall, sent her nerves skittering. She'd be lucky if she got any sleep at all.

As it was, she'd been lying in bed beneath the sheet, going over the evening, trying to get a grip on her emotions—emotions churned up by Jackson Slade *and* his daughter.

Once Tori had loosened up, her energy hadn't flagged. She'd still been wound up when they'd come home, and had danced, and sung and shaken her bottom as she'd climbed the stairs to bed, an entirely different child.

It had taken a cup of sweetened herbal tea, sipped while they'd sat in the middle of Tori's bed, reading aloud a chapter of one of her Nancy Drew books, before Sunny had gotten the child settled and tucked in, with Simba and Twinkie snuggled beside her.

Of course, Sunny had had to play referee with the

animals before peace and quiet had been established. The cat had been put out that Simba was in *her* spot, but Simba, with his everybody-loves-me personality, didn't notice. That trait could wear down even the strongest foe, and Twinkie finally acknowledged that she'd lost the battle. She'd curled up inches away, glaring at the dog, who was entirely too big to sleep on the bed in any case.

The heart clincher, Sunny thought now, had been when Tori had wrapped her small arms around Sunny's neck and whispered, "Thank you for letting me be a Sweetheart. You're the best friend I've ever had."

The adoration in the child's eyes had melted Sunny's heart. The realization that came had nearly buckled her knees.

She'd fallen in love with that little girl.

And darn it all, she could deny it until the cows came home, but she was still in love with Jack Slade.

What a mess. She pulled the sheet over her head, but hiding didn't banish the swirl of unwanted emotions. It only added to the mix.

Folding the sheet back to her waist, she stared at the crib-size quilt that hung on the wall as decoration, wondering if Doris Slade had stitched it for Jack or his brother, Linc.

The floorboards in the hallway creaked, and Sunny froze. Adrenaline shot through her when her bedroom door opened quietly, the light from the hall slicing across the wooden floor.

Jack.

She held her breath for a moment, wondered what he would do. He stood in the doorway for a long time, watching her—though she knew he couldn't see her clearly in the dark. When he gave no indication whether he intended to come or go, Sunny decided to help him out.

"I'm awake." She sat up to turn on the lamp, but when she flicked the switch, nothing happened. It was controlled by the one near the door.

"Do you want the light on?" Jack asked.

"I'll get it in a minute." The answer was automatic, and silly, she realized, since he was standing right next to the switch. She was used to doing things for herself, rarely asked others for help. "I'm still wound up from dinner, I suppose. I thought I might read awhile."

He hit the light switch and the lamp glowed softly. "Did everything go all right?"

"Yes. Tori had a good time." Now that Sunny could see him clearly, she noticed that he looked tired—emotionally tired.

"I just checked on her. She's out like a bear in hibernation. She has fried-chicken grease in her hair. You wouldn't happen to know anything about that, would you?"

"Nope, not a thing." The droll fib tripped right off her tongue. The Texas Sweethearts maintained loyalty at all times. "I imagine it'll wash out."

"I imagine." He moved across the room and stood by the side of the bed. "Thanks for taking care of her for me."

"She's a wonderful girl, Jack. We all enjoyed her company."

"I was surprised she stayed. She doesn't usually go with strangers."

"I'm not exactly a stranger." He was standing so close she could smell the aroma of soap on his skin.

"It's… I don't know. Her social world is pretty

much narrowed to Cora, Beau and me—at least when school's out for the summer. She's not comfortable with the men on the ranch.''

"I noticed that when Duane came over before we left."

"He's tried several times to get her to warm up to him. I feel bad. He lost his wife and daughter a while back, and he misses having a family.''

"Oh, that's awful. What happened?''

"He didn't say and I didn't ask. I hadn't even known he was married.''

"Has he worked for you long?''

"Two or three months, but I've known him a long time. His daddy and mine were drinking buddies. When George Keegan went off with another woman, my father roped Duane in as his replacement. After that, Duane took up rodeo and traveled the circuit until a bull got him and put him out of commission for that kind of work.''

"So you gave him a job." She'd heard that about Jack—that he'd lend a hand to anyone in need. In a way it was surprising. This town hadn't always been nice to him, had judged him by his father's actions. Here he was, though, a successful rancher, a reserve deputy, a man who looked like a handsome hellion, yet took care of his family and the families of others, as well.

He shrugged. "He's a friend. Besides, there's always plenty of work on the ranch. How's your leg?'' He started to draw back the sheet covering her.

She slapped a hand down, stopping him. "What's with this doctoring obsession all of a sudden?''

"No obsession. You were injured on my property. It's in my best interests to follow up.''

"For pity's sake, I'm not going to sue."

"Good. Now, can I look?"

The patient determination in his gaze never wavered, and she didn't have to be hit over the head with a plucked chicken to figure out his intent. If she didn't let him have his way, he'd stand there all night.

Hissing out a breath, she swished aside the sheet. She wore an oversize T-shirt that was plenty modest, so exposing herself wasn't a worry.

"There's nothing to see. The wound's covered." Sort of. Humidity and adhesive weren't a good match. The corners of the square patch had curled and lifted.

He shook his head. "What'd you do with the stuff I set out for you to use after your shower?"

"I decided to go with something smaller."

"Obviously, smaller isn't working. Stay right there."

Her jaw dropped, a smart remark on the tip of her tongue, but she was left staring at his back as he walked away, the untucked hem of his shirt drawing her eyes to his excellent backside. Where in the world did he think she would go in the middle of the night? She was in her assigned bed in his guest room.

And when, she'd like to know, had he become such a nag? That wasn't a trait she would usually put up with.

Well, hell. If it would make him happy, she'd wrap the damn scrape.

She waited impatiently while he gathered supplies from his bathroom. Yet when he walked back into the room, instead of handing her the first-aid kit, he sat on the edge of the mattress.

Before she could object, he ripped off the flimsy bandage.

"Ouch!" She glared at him. "See? It was sticking just fine."

"On one side." He applied more salve and a fresh gauze pad. "If this is how you dress wounds on animals, I hope you have good insurance."

That got her back up. "I'm an excellent vet."

"I know. But you're a lousy patient. Lift up." With his palm cupping the underside of her leg, he encouraged her to bend her knee to give him access, then began winding the soft bandage around her thigh, smoothing it with his fingers as he went.

Chills prickled her skin—from his touch and from two words. *I know.* The compliment had been simple and straightforward. A matter-of-fact confirmation that he sincerely respected her skills.

She stared at the top of his head as he bent over his task. His dark hair, fresh-smelling from his shower, beckoned her to reach out and touch.

And she might have done just that if an onslaught of spine-tingling desire hadn't paralyzed her.

After three loops with the bandage, his fingers grazing her inner thigh on each revolution, Sunny was ready to combust.

"That's good enough," she mumbled, surprised her vocal cords even worked. Her heart drummed in her ears and acute awareness shivered beneath her skin. If he didn't take his hands off her in the next two seconds, she might do or say something that wouldn't be good for either one of them.

The stretch bandage clung on its own, but he fastened a piece of tape at the edges. Then he simply sat there, his hands resting gently atop the newly bandaged wound, his long fingers lying idle on her inner thigh.

His stillness was more erotic than a full-out seduction.

Longing built inside her, from a whisper to a roaring scream. Memory flashed in her mind—of another time, another place, with Jack's fingers touching her softly…inching upward by exquisitely electrifying degrees.

As she recalled the vivid moment, Jack looked up. And caught her staring.

There was no way to hide the pulse beating frantically in her neck, or the flush that heated her skin. So she simply indulged herself and held his gaze.

His eyes shimmered in a way she remembered well, the eyes of a man who knew how to read a woman's desire, who had the confidence and skill to gift her— brand her—with the kind of touching that would spoil her for every other relationship.

She should know.

His hands moved to her hips. Slowly, oh, so slowly, he leaned toward her.

Her heart sang out, *Yes. Please kiss me. It's been so long.* But at the last crucial second, her mind shouted, *No.*

She brought her hand up between them, placed it in the center of his chest. "Jack. I don't want this."

He stopped immediately, his gaze holding hers. "Your eyes say different."

"I know." There was too much between them to deny it. "What I should say is that it isn't good for me."

"Why?"

She looked away, unresolved emotions dousing the flames of desire.

He put a finger under her chin, turned her face back to his. "Why?"

"Because you broke my heart." The words had simply spilled out. Damn it. She hadn't wanted to admit that to him. Not after all this time.

It was as though she'd thrown a bucket of ice water on him. He drew in a breath and pulled back, his eyes sad.

"I know, Sunny. And I'm sorry."

The immediate, utterly sincere apology surprised her. "No excuses or explanations?"

"There aren't any." He ran a hand through his hair, the action both agitated and weary. "And I shouldn't have gotten out of line here."

Technically, she had started it with her I-want-your-body gaze, but encouraging that particular debate didn't seem like a good idea.

He looked like a man shouldering a heavy weight that at any minute might shift and tumble, leaving his world in ruins. How did he bear up under it all—the worry over his daughter, his beef operation, the lives and livelihoods of his employees, the hours he gave to the community?

A reserve deputy, she thought in wonder. Ten years ago, most folks in town would have expected him to break the law, not uphold it. But most people hadn't bothered to know the real Jackson Slade.

Reaching out, she touched his arm. They both needed a distraction. "How did the tanker spill go?"

He accepted the change of subject with barely a blink. "Messy. We had to call out a medevac helicopter to take the truck driver to the hospital. I'll be surprised if he pulls through."

Sunny knew she should tell Jack good-night and not

tempt fate, but the rough emotion in his voice had her mind and her heart warring once more.

This time, her heart won.

She had never been able to resist anyone who needed to be fixed.

Patting the mattress beside her, she said, "Since I'm not sleepy and you look pretty keyed up, why don't you prop yourself up here and tell me about it."

"That might not be a good idea in light of what nearly happened just now."

The kiss. She gave a flippant shrug. "'Nearly' doesn't count. Chalk it up to curiosity. Who knows, tomorrow I might be kicking myself for stopping you."

He blinked. She'd clearly caught him off guard. Then his lips slowly canted in an innocently sexy smile that Red Riding Hood would have recognized in an instant.

"No reason to resort to violence, sugar bear. I'll be happy to oblige that curiosity."

"I was talking about *your* curiosity, cowboy." *Fibber.* "Besides, you look like you could really use a friend." She flicked her hair behind her ear, tried to keep her tone light. "Someone once told me I'm a pretty good one."

His eyes softened, acknowledging the shared memory. That "someone" had been him. For a long moment, he stared at her like a grateful man who'd finally fought through the fog of amnesia.

"I've missed you, Sunny."

Those four quietly reverent, simply stated words touched her heart.

He covered her with the sheet. Then he scooted up

on the bed next to her, propped his head against the
headboard and stretched out his long legs.

"Okay. Start at the beginning and tell me all about
the truck mishap."

His lips twitched. "You're such a ghoul."

"Of course I am. That's why I aced surgical training. One of the biggest guys in the class fainted dead
away when we opened up the belly of a donkey."
Sunny wasn't treating the devastation of the accident
lightly. But she knew Jack, knew he would walk
around for days with emotions bottled inside him if he
didn't talk them out.

And so he did, his deep voice hushed in deference
to the subject matter.

If she believed in magic, she'd swear the years had
suddenly melted away. As she had countless times in
the past, she listened while he purged his mind and
soul.

He was a tough guy, but he took sadness and injury
to heart. It was one of the things that had made her
fall in love with him all those years ago.

Typically, men internalized and women went batty
prying details out of them. It hadn't been that way with
Sunny and Jack. When they were young, they'd talked
for hours, about anything and everything. She'd
thought she knew him so well....

Then, in a matter of seconds, their lives had fallen
apart. The way it had for that trucker tonight when a
careless driver had misjudged his distance and tried to
pass. The trucker had had to make a split-second decision in panic and disbelief, desperately yanking the
wheel, steering clear, fighting to stay on the road, only
to crash and burn in the end, alive but gravely injured.

Metaphorically, that pretty much summed up Sunny's collision with fate ten years ago.

Jack reached over and squeezed her hand. She jolted, realized she'd zoned out for a minute.

"Am I putting you to sleep?" he asked.

She smiled and carefully slid her hand from beneath his. "You know better than that." He was staring at the ceiling, but she could tell by the relaxed set of his shoulders that talking had helped.

"Thanks for listening…and for remembering."

"You're welcome. That's what pals are for."

He shifted his head against the pillow, and studied her for a long moment. "Sometimes when I look at you, I forget what's behind us. I know we can't go back and I know we've both moved in different directions in our lives…." His voice trailed off as though he wasn't sure how to continue.

Her pulse skittered at the new subject, a topic she hadn't anticipated. She nodded, part of her glad that he'd acknowledged their differences and another part sad that they had ended up this way.

"I've got regrets, Sun," he said softly, "but I have Tori. And I'll never regret her."

"She's a great kid." Sunny shouldn't ask, shouldn't dredge up the past. But the door was open and she doubted she'd get a better opportunity. "Since we're on a roll here, I guess I've always wondered what Lanette had that I didn't."

"Don't do that, sugar bear. What happened was my fault, not yours. You were perfect."

"So perfect you married someone else?"

Jack ran a hand over his face, the quiet unsteadiness in her voice ripping at him like barbed wire gouging exposed skin.

"I screwed up. If you'd stuck around that day, I would have told you that Lanette was kissing me—I wasn't kissing her back. You just happened to walk in at the exact moment she jumped me."

"You're a big guy. It's a little hard to understand why you didn't turn your head or hold her away."

"In hindsight I realized I probably could have done that. But she caught me by surprise." He didn't think he would ever forget the look of betrayal in Sunny's eyes when she'd seen him with Lanette plastered against his body.

He'd wanted to defend himself, had almost done just that. But she'd called him a son of a bitch, whirled and run. His own pain had kept him silent, but he'd been plenty ticked off at her, too.

Sunny was the first person in his life he'd trusted with his secrets, with his true self, with his heart.

And she'd let him down.

She hadn't given him the benefit of the doubt, hadn't let him explain. He'd worked himself into a state, told himself that if she'd really loved him, she would have stuck by his side, believed in him.

Years of being "that Slade kid," of expecting to be slapped in the face because he was a misfit, had colored his thinking, and he'd let her walk away. All he'd been able to see was a red haze of righteousness because she hadn't trusted him. Because she'd judged him instantly, tried, sentenced and hanged him without ever giving him a chance to mount a defense.

Stubbornness had kept him from going after her. And by the time he'd cooled down enough to try to mend fences, he'd run up against a solid wall of protective family members and friends, who'd told him that Sunny was gone, but wouldn't tell him where.

What had come after that was pure stupidity and pride. He had to take full responsibility for his actions. No one had held a gun to his head and made him drink that bottle of Scotch.

"If the kiss didn't mean anything," Sunny said, "why did you go ahead and sleep with her? Marry her?"

"I slept with her because I was mad at every sorry minute of my life up until that point. I was a fool and I was flat-out drunk." He heard Sunny inhale sharply, but he kept talking, even as shame tightened like a fist in his belly.

"Lanette showed up with more determination than a drunken, self-pitying twenty-two-year-old guy could stand tough against. You were gone. I rationalized that I wasn't cheating on you, that you leaving town was your way of breaking up, and I just said what the hell. That's not an excuse, Sunny. I took those drinks, I made that choice. I regretted it like hell the next morning."

"You drank?"

He wondered if she'd heard anything past that admission. His mother had died in a car accident with his father at the wheel. Drunk. Jack had sworn he'd never be like Russell Slade. As a teen, guys had needled him about choosing soda over alcohol, but he never let it phase him.

"First and last time in my life. I haven't had anything since."

"That was my fault, wasn't it?" Sunny gripped the edge of the sheet, guilt rearing its ugly head. She'd known how important sobriety was to him, and their breakup had obviously opened the dam, drowning his control.

"No. It was mine. I made the choice. And it was a hell of a wake-up call for me. I had a lot of issues to work through, and I needed to do it alone. But I couldn't concentrate, not knowing where you'd gone. I badgered your mother until she finally told me you'd enrolled in college. She wouldn't tell me which college or what state."

"I'd asked her not to."

He nodded. "That's one of the reasons I didn't push. I decided not to distract you, to give us both some space to cool off. I'd intended to find you, try to make things right, thinking I had a better chance once the initial emotions settled down. Then a month later, Lanette told me she was pregnant. The one thing my mom had drilled into my head and Linc's was to take responsibility for our actions. I married her the next day."

"Oh."

His gut burned like leather stuck to a branding iron, but he had to finish this. "Your friends wouldn't have anything to do with me after you left, and I didn't blame them. They're loyal to you. But I ran into Donetta one day, and she blasted me, said some things that I hadn't considered, made me realize how self-absorbed I'd been."

"What did she say?"

"I don't even remember now." He remembered exactly. *How could you think her emotions and reactions were only anger? Are you blind? Or just plain stupid? You've been her future for so long, Jack—how would you expect her to cope? Sure, she wanted to be a vet, but the main thing she wanted, what you led her to believe she could expect, was to be your wife. And today, I had to call my best friend and shatter her heart the rest of the way by telling her you married Lanette McGreavy and are expecting a kid.*

"I just know that I let my pride stand in the way that night when I should have come after you. I've never deliberately hurt anyone, Sunny. But I hurt you. And if I could go back and change things, I would. I'm sorry."

The utter sincerity in his voice moved her. She reached over and slid her hand beneath his. "Me, too, Jack."

The rain had started again, tapping against the closed window. The air conditioner kicked on, whistling softly through the vent.

Talking about the past forced her to look at it in a different light, one that wasn't colored by her emotions. They'd both had a part in the split. She had run away, stunned and devastated. But deep down in her romantic heart, she'd expected him to chase after her. As the hours had passed and he hadn't even called, she'd assumed he'd made his choice—and she wasn't it.

It had been the blackest moment in her life.

From there, the night became a blur—sobbing on Tracy Lynn's father's shoulder while her girlfriends helplessly gathered around; snatching clothes and toiletry items and shoving them into the trunk and back seat of her car as Mama dogged her footsteps, offering advice that had only made the pain worse.

Sunny had driven to California with no guarantee she could even get into UC Davis—nor had she considered finances. She'd been too numb for rational thought. But Tracy Lynn's father, Mayor Randolph, had had a powerful contact. On the strength of his phone call and Sunny's impressive four-point-three average, not only was she accepted, but she was offered a sizable grant to cover tuition.

The ensuing years had been rough, but her career had made the struggle worthwhile.

Perhaps she and Jack had simply been too young to handle the rough bumps that invariably arose in relationships. Maybe going their separate ways had been for the best.

At nineteen, her heart and mind had been overflowing with love, with images of a fairy-tale house and white picket fence. With her young emotions running that strong, would she have set aside her goal and dream of becoming a veterinarian in favor of being a wife and mother?

She'd been so totally focused on Jack. Looking back now, she felt frightened at the choices she might have made.

The air conditioner shut off, leaving the room in silence. Neither of them had spoken in the past few moments. There didn't seem to be any more to say.

After ten years, she finally understood the sequence of events that had nearly destroyed her.

But that understanding didn't change anything.

Jack had invested his entire life in his Texas ranch and she'd invested hers in her California career. There wasn't a suture strong enough to hold such opposing seams together.

She glanced over at him. He was so quiet she wondered if he'd fallen asleep. His shirt skimmed his flat stomach. His long legs were crossed at the ankles, his feet bare. He was the epitome of maleness, tall and strong and so sexy he made her ache.

Despite the past, there was still a powerful chemistry between them. Making love had been one of the things she and Jack had done best. She hadn't found that kind of fever with anyone else over the years—not even Michael, whom she'd nearly married.

Ten years was a long time to go without full satisfaction from a man.

Today had been a physical and emotional roller coaster. To escape into the ecstasy of raw, elemental passion would be so easy. The man lying beside her was an expert lover.

She could roll over just a bit and be on top of him, press against him, kiss the scar on his brow, the lids of his piercing blue eyes, his sensual lips, his strong, smooth-shaven chin...and let him take it from there.

She wasn't nineteen anymore. She knew that sex didn't have to lead to commitment—which neither was in a position to give.

As though he could feel her gaze, read her thoughts, he opened his eyes and turned his head.

And just that quickly, her pulse stampeded and her hands trembled. He stared at her the way no other man could, making her feel sexy and attractive and bold.

She'd never had vacation sex before. That was what it would be if she gave in to her desire. She would be here only a few weeks. What could it hurt? The idea took hold, grew in her mind, enticed her.

She shifted toward him, winced when the mattress connected with her sore leg—

"I've got to get out of here," Jack said suddenly, scooting off the bed in one swift move. "Neither of us will be worth a damn in the morning if we don't get some sleep."

Holy crud. He'd leaped up so fast that it was a wonder she hadn't fallen flat on her face on the mattress. She knew he'd seen the hunger in her eyes, and the last thing she'd expected was for him to jump like an Angus goosed by a cattle prod.

"Thanks again for taking care of Tori."

"You're welcome again. Good night, Jack." She was proud of the steadiness in her voice. As soon as the bedroom door closed behind him, she flopped back against the pillow and gave a mental scream.

She ought to be happy that at least one of them had had enough control to keep a level head. They seemed to alternate—she'd be strong one minute, then he'd be strong the next.

Lord help them if they ended up synchronizing their weak moments while she was still in Texas.

Chapter Eleven

Sunny lifted her head from the microscope and rubbed at the kink in her neck, wondering why the hell she wasn't spending her vacation at a posh spa. There, saints with clever fingers could pamper and massage her body until she was boneless with bliss.

Instead of aromatherapy oils, she was surrounded by the lingering scents of flea powder, antiseptic and animals here in Hope Valley's deserted veterinarian clinic. The smells were familiar—and blissful in their own way. Because Sunny loved anything and everything that had to do with animals

Now, if someone would give her a massage and some drops for eye strain, she'd be in good shape.

For the past two days, she'd worked beside Jack, collecting more samples, not only from the cattle but from the water and the feed supply.

Ever since the incident with the cow kick, though, Jack had hovered like a mother hawk guarding her nest. Oh, he thought he was being inconspicuous and clever, but every time she turned around, she was tripping over him. And tripping over a sexy man wearing a Stetson and chaps wasn't doing a thing to calm her libido.

A libido that had been in overdrive since the night Jack had lain in bed with her.

She might have appreciated his control at the time. As the hours had passed, however, and her sensitized body had shown no signs of relaxing, she'd been working herself into a fine sexual snit.

Damn it, vacation sex was a hell of a good idea.

Yet the tall, virile, too-sexy-for-his-pants cowboy ignored her signals as though she were invisible.

Well, she couldn't be *too* invisible; otherwise she'd have been able to evade his maddeningly protective bossiness: *I'll do that, Sunny. Watch that hole, Sunny. Why don't you sit over there in the shade and rest, Sunny? Here, now, sugar bear, don't be lifting that feed sack. It's too heavy.*

She'd nearly swung around and clobbered him with the damn sack. Didn't the man have his own work to do, instead of meddling in hers?

Frustrated, she'd packed her supplies in the Suburban and driven into town to the peacefully empty veterinarian clinic to use the lab. Here she was in *her* arena, where she could lose herself in the complicated puzzle of science. The facility was organized and nicely equipped, though not as well as the lab she worked at in California.

Since the massage fairies didn't show up, she leaned back over the binocular microscope and prepared to ruin her twenty-twenty vision through excessive and prolonged strain.

She'd been checking serum samples for three hours now, and so far every test she'd run had turned up nonreactive.

That was the good news.

The results, however, didn't shed any light on Jack's mysteriously dead cattle.

"Yoo-hoo. Is anyone here?"

Sunny jumped. The smear she'd been holding beneath the microscope skidded onto the counter.

Adrenaline zinging through her veins, she shot up from the stool and started toward the front of the clinic, where she came face-to-face with a birdlike woman holding a little poodle.

"I saw your car. You're the new vet, aren't you?"

"Well, I—"

"Debbie's been limping something fierce lately. Poor baby, she cries if I set her down."

Debbie was a teacup poodle. In a cattle town, most people had big dogs or working dogs. But this pampered pup was adorable.

Technically, Sunny wasn't Hope Valley's new veterinarian, but the older woman and the puff ball she held in her age-spotted hands were peering at her as though she were the last canteen of water on a drought-plagued range.

"Bring her over and I'll have a look, Mrs.—"

"Drucilla Taggatt." She beamed, crinkling the corners of her eyes. "Folks call me Dru."

"Nice to meet you. I'm Dr. Carmichael."

"I know. I heard all about you over at the beauty shop. Not that I gossip with the likes of Millicent Lloyd and Darla Pam Kirkwell, you understand. Why, Darla Pam ought to tend to her own business, if you ask me. She's got herself a good man—one who's been devoted to her for over thirty years. You'd think she'd stay home and appreciate what's hers, instead of trying to lure every man who's got a set of equipment in his pants…if you know what I mean."

"Mmm." Best not to get drawn into the middle of *that* potential catfight.

Debbie yapped once and whined when Sunny lifted her from Dru's arms. "Here, now. No need to fuss," she murmured. "Let's just have a gander at these dainty feet. What do you say?" As she spoke, she checked the dog's paws and stroked her fur, examining and soothing at the same time. Years had passed since she'd tended an animal so tiny. This was a nice change. "Now I see what's the matter. You've been playing outside, haven't you, Deb."

"She has?" Dru squeaked in bewilderment. "Well, I mean, she goes out the doggie door to do her business, but she never dawdles. I've a nice bed of petunias and zinnias, and a soft patch of grass for her."

"I'm sure you have a beautiful yard. Debbie just picked up a small stone." Because it seemed important, Sunny added, "It could have happened anywhere—perhaps on one of your trips to town?" She swabbed the little dog's paw with antiseptic.

"Why, I believe you could be right. I've told the city council that we need better maintenance people over at the senior citizens' center. I teach aerobics at the center to a bunch of old coots."

Sunny glanced up and quickly masked her astonishment. Mrs. Taggatt had to be pushing ninety.

She smiled, then spread the pads of Debbie's paw and plucked out the stone with a pair of tweezers. Dru's head kept blocking the light as she scrutinized every step of her beloved little dog's procedure. They were practically cheek-to-cheek, the delicate scent of lavender wafting off the older woman's powdered skin.

"You're very gentle," Dru commented. "Debbie

never would sit still like this for Doc Levin. I suspect part of it was that young tart he took up with. Debbie didn't like her a bit.''

Sunny was sure she didn't need to hear these details, but Dru chattered on.

''She worked as his receptionist, you know. Lucinda was her name. Twenty-three years younger than him, too. He was worse than a strutting peacock—showing her off all over town like he'd found the fountain of youth. He even started coming to my aerobics class, but in my opinion, he'd have been better off to have one of those vanity doctors over in Dallas stick a big tube in him and muck out the fat.''

Muck out the fat? Sunny hadn't heard of that technique.

She wasn't keen on encouraging gossip, but something had been nagging at her while she'd been alone in the clinic.

Jack's cattle began dying after Stanley Levin disappeared.

''Do you know why he left so suddenly?'' She palpated Debbie's paws and checked for abnormalities. ''I can't imagine a professional just abandoning his clinic.''

''Oh, he didn't own this place. Everything in here was bought and paid for by Millicent Lloyd.''

''I wasn't aware of that,'' Sunny stated. Surely her mother or Jack would have told her. Especially Anna, who'd made several none-too-subtle hints that Sunny should step into Levin's shoes while she was here— that it would be the *nice* thing to do.

But Sunny already had a job, a career. And it paid more than triple what this clinic probably brought in.

''It's not common knowledge. Millie's real closemouthed over what she does with her money. As for why Dr. Levin disappeared—that's anybody's guess. He owes money all over town." Dru leaned close and lowered her voice as though fearing someone would overhear. "I think Lucinda got him into experimenting with drugs. Then again, maybe she conked him in the head and sank him in the river."

Well, that was a chilling thought. "Did anyone look for him after he left?"

"Not as far as I know. He didn't have any kin in town. No real friends, either. Before that woman came, he just doctored animals and went about his business."

Sunny decided she'd have Storm check into it. As awful as it sounded, she'd prefer to believe Jack's cattle were the victims of foul play rather than plagued with disease. Then again, maybe she was merely grasping at straws.

The most frustrating cases to deal with were herds that were asymptomatic. Some strains of bacteria were sleepers, hiding away in cells where standard tests wouldn't detect them.

A careless dismissal by an owner or a vet could cause national chaos.

And Sunny certainly didn't want her name at the bottom of a health certification form if that happened. She'd have to kiss her career goodbye.

She scratched Debbie's tummy, then lifted the tiny dog off the table and gave her a cuddle, just for the pure pleasure of it.

"You're all better now, pup." Passing the quivering dog back to Dru, she said, "There's no infection, just a bit of a bruise. Her paw might be tender for a couple of days, but she'll be just fine."

"Oh, thank you, dear. I'm so relieved. I thought you'd have to do surgery."

"Not this time. Do you need anything else? Is she current with her shots?"

"Oh, yes. I mark the dates on the calendar. I want to keep my girl healthy and happy. What do I owe you?"

I have no idea. "Um, don't worry about it now. Just write down your name and address out front and we'll...bill you."

Sunny didn't mind helping out in a pinch, and certainly wouldn't turn her back on an animal in need. But taking on this private practice wasn't feasible, no matter how often her mother brought up the subject.

Time was slipping through her fingers like fine grains of Texas silt. She couldn't ask for an extension on her vacation because of the seminar on large-animal infectious diseases she was due to conduct in Washington the first week of August.

How ironic. She was considered the best in her field, a virtual wonder in the industry to have attained this stature at such a young age. Yet on the case that mattered most, one that could affect her entire hometown and the people she loved, she was stumped.

She woke each morning with a sense of dread that this would be the day they'd find another dead cow—or mass death.

More than anything, she didn't want to be the one forced to call in reinforcements—to seriously damage Jack's future.

WHEN SUNNY GOT BACK to the ranch, Jack and Tori were near the barn, bending over something on the ground. She couldn't tell what, because Scotty was in her way, holding the reins of Jack's saddled horse.

At the sound of the engine, Tori jumped up, then sprinted toward the Suburban, her blond ponytail flying, her face ravaged by tears.

Panic, swift and fierce, came out of nowhere, engulfing her before she could think. *Dear God, don't let it be Simba.*

She slammed the truck into Park and leaped out, then barreled straight at Tori and swept the girl into her arms.

"What? Sugar, calm down. What's wrong? Where's Simba?"

"H-he's in the b-barn." Tori sniffed and took a breath. "Daddy said he should stay there 'cause he was licking and trying to help the bird."

Utter relief made Sunny dizzy. Her brain finally cleared enough to focus. "What bird?"

"The one that mean old stray cat got. It's hurt. Can you fix it? It bit Daddy."

"Who did? The cat or the bird?"

"The bird."

She set Tori down but held on to her hand. Even though she knew the little girl's tears weren't over Simba, her own legs still felt like overcooked linguini. "Let's go see."

When they reached the barn, Scotty had taken the horse into a stable and Jack was trying to corral the bird, muttering a string of swear words as it continued to evade him.

He looked up with a strained, exasperated smile. "I'm not having much luck here."

Sunny crouched beside him. The bright green bird

flapped one wing, then listed drunkenly, making one heck of a flutter but only managing to move in a circle.

"It's a wild parrot." She scooted closer and rested on her knees.

"Careful," he warned. "Don't let that pretty exterior fool you. It bites."

"It's scared." Carefully, expertly, she managed to wrap her hands around the parrot's body, gently folding its wings. Part of the beak was broken off, but the blunted edge indicated that was an old injury. "Okay, buddy, okay."

She stroked and soothed and held the bird close to her chest, felt its tiny heart hammering. Evidently, this was her day to brush up on her small-animal veterinary skills.

Examining a frightened, injured bird wasn't easy, but after a while, either sensing Sunny could be trusted—or feeling just flat-out exhausted—the parrot finally gave up the fight, allowing her to assess the damage.

"The wing's definitely broken." That presented a challenge, since her equipment was better suited for working on large animals.

"Can you fix it?" Tori asked. She was kneeling next to her dad, leaning forward to peer at the bird. Her tears had dried; now her brown eyes showed compassion and worry.

"I think so, but I'll require a couple of assistants. Do you mind parting with that rubber band in your hair, sugar?"

Without a word, Tori pulled it off, causing her blond hair to tumble past her waist.

"Good girl. Hang on to it for a few minutes. Jack, I'll need you to hold the bird."

"Are you crazy? That beak's lethal."

"It is not. It's broken. Just hush up and put on your gloves." Normally, even *she* wouldn't be handling a wild bird with bare hands, but she didn't tell him that. With the parrot having a blunted beak, she didn't imagine anyone would get too bloody in the fray. And besides, Jack's annoyance was too endearing to resist.

He snatched his heavy suede gloves out of his back pocket and pulled them on. "Damn right I'll put on my gloves. Now what?"

"Now I'll gently shift the parrot into your hands and you'll work on putting a little honey in your voice."

His eyes narrowed, but he held out his cupped hands as she transferred the bird. As soon as she let go, it immediately tried to bite him.

"See?" he said, sounding gravely put-upon.

"Don't squeeze."

"I'm not. But if I don't hold it tight, it'll get away. It's a better escape artist than Houdini."

"Do you want me to hold him, Daddy?"

Sunny raised a brow, waited for his decision, biting the inside of her cheek to keep from grinning. His masculine feathers were good and ruffled now. She recalled her mother's words about men and their fragile egos. Maybe Mama wasn't so old-fashioned after all.

"I've got it, darlin'," he grumbled.

Sunny worked as quickly as she could, since she didn't have any meds to relax the bird. She doubted there was even a conversion table in her medical books that cross-referenced bovine tranquilizer with the correct dosage for a parrot. Guessing wasn't an option. The bird would probably relax right into cardiac arrest.

Using one of the healthy bones in the bird's wing as a splint for the broken one, she carefully aligned them like toothpicks, then wrapped Tori's hair band around them both. Every so often, the parrot craned its head around and tried to take a chunk out of Jack's gloved finger. He didn't utter a sound.

"That should do it." She gently scooped the parrot from Jack's palms and stroked a finger over the brightly colored feathers.

He hissed out a breath. "The thing acts like a spoiled house cat when you hold it."

"I've got magic hands."

His gaze snapped to her. He'd told her that when she was younger. When they'd made love. *You've got magic hands, sugar bear. You put a spell on me when you touch me like that.*

Sunny broke eye contact. "Uh, do you have some kind of cage we can put the parrot in while it heals?"

He stood, tugged at his hat and looked around, as if expecting a cage to materialize out of thin air.

Like magic.

Great. Now the word and the memory were going to stick in her mind, like that vacation-sex thing, keeping her up at night. Awake and wanting.

She was sorely tempted to dunk herself in the water trough.

"What about the one in Grandma's garden?" Tori asked.

Jack's mother had passed away well before Tori's birth, but he'd obviously told his daughter about the grandmother she'd never known. Sunny could picture father and daughter tending roses and azaleas while he recounted stories of a woman who'd died too young.

"I imagine that'd work," Jack said, looking toward

the front of the house, where colorful flowers thrived despite the hot July sun. "I was going to put plants in it, but we might as well use it for the purpose it's meant for."

He strode toward the house and Tori leaned close to Sunny. "Daddy likes to go to yard sales. That's where he got the birdcage." As she spoke, she gently ran a finger over the parrot's head. The bird flinched, but then settled down and let her touch.

"You're very good with animals," Sunny commented.

"They talk to me with their eyes."

Sunny didn't find that statement strange. From the time she was young, she'd felt a connection with animals that defied explanation.

"I knew you could fix Dini," Tori murmured.

"Dini?"

She grinned. "Like Houdini. Just shorter."

Sunny had noticed that Tori assigned her animals shortened names—like Beauty for the beautiful foal, and now Dini. She had no idea why the thought clicked in her head, but it almost seemed that the little girl made the easiest, quickest choices, as if she didn't trust her imagination or allow herself to think much further than the moment.

"Can we keep Dini?"

"Only until his wing is healed, sugar. He looks like a pet, but he's used to being wild and flying free. He'd be sad if he had to stay in a cage for the rest of his life."

"I don't want him to be sad. Do you think he could learn to talk?"

"Oh, wouldn't that be a mess." Sunny laughed, and the bird squirmed in her hands for a minute, then tucked his head down and grew still. "Can't you just imagine a flock of wild parrots sitting on someone's backyard fence, then flying around town repeating the gossip they'd heard?"

Tori giggled. "Probably people would get real mad at one another. If Dini came to our yard, he'd be saying Beau's cuss words."

"And begging pardon," Sunny added, tickled at the prospect. "So, how did Dini manage to put himself in the cat's path?"

"He flew too low and hit the side of the barn. He probably got dirt in his eye and couldn't see. I thought he was in a coma or something, because he just sat on the ground. Then he started to walk, and that old tom ran right over and grabbed him in his mouth. It scared me so bad that I cried and yelled, and he dropped the bird."

"You didn't get scratched, did you?"

"No. Daddy came running."

"Good." Evidently, this bird was the klutz in his flock, with a broken beak, poor navigational and reaction skills.

And maybe she was wrong about Tori's imagination; maybe she was snatching scenarios out of the air because she couldn't stand not knowing the answer to a puzzle. That and her innate need to fix anything broken.

"So, have you been checking on Violet and Beauty?" she asked.

"Oh, yes. Beauty grew last night. I just know it. I tried to put a mark on the stall—the way Beau does for me on the kitchen wall. It shows how much taller I'm getting. But Beauty wouldn't stand still, and I didn't know if I should measure from the top of her ears or just her head. Plus, she kept wiggling her ears."

"Those wily ears'll goof you up every time. When we get Dini settled, I'll show you how we measure so you can keep a good record of her growth."

AS JACK ROUNDED THE HOUSE, carrying the birdcage, what he saw caused his steps to slow and his heart to stutter.

Sunny and Tori, looking like mother and daughter with their blond heads close together, sat on the ground, Tori talking earnestly and gesturing with her hands, Sunny listening.

He'd never seen his daughter respond to anyone— not even her own mother—the way she did to Sunny.

He cautioned himself not to get caught up in emotions and lose sight of reality. He appreciated the attention she'd lavished on Tori, was moved beyond words as his daughter began to emerge from her shell, but at the same time their closeness made him nervous.

Sunny wasn't here to stay.

He had an idea that his daughter was already forming an emotional attachment that could easily break her heart. Hell, he fully understood and sympathized, because he was doing the same thing. To be around Sunny for more than five minutes and not be captivated by her charm and want her there all the time was damn hard.

She was as petite as ever, and hardly looked a day older than in the picture he still carried in his wallet of the two of them at her high-school prom. But there were changes in her, too. She held her cards close to her chest, kept him off balance, maneuvered him into talking about himself, yet didn't offer many details about her life.

For her to have come to his ranch, to be confronted every day with a tangible reminder of his past with Lanette, must have been difficult. He'd hurt Sunny badly, and even though he'd apologized, the words couldn't erase what had been done. Scars never faded completely.

Sunny had shown class and strength by coming here, parking herself under his roof, working like crazy to save his hide—or determine if it needed saving.

He would cut off his right arm before he'd hurt her again—in any way. But he was walking a shaky fence here.

He was trying to be a decent guy and respect whatever limits she set, but damned if he could read her signals. First she'd told him he wasn't good for her, and then she'd changed horses in the middle of the stream and started looking at him as if he were dessert and the only one invited to her party.

It bugged him that he couldn't figure her out—and that he was still so attracted to her he could hardly see straight.

But damn it all, she had him as confused as a goat on Astro Turf. He ought to just toss his good intentions out the window and take her to bed, which was what he'd been aching to do from the minute he'd set eyes on her standing by his landing strip with her goofy-looking dog.

He watched her touch her forehead to Tori's, still cradling the vicious bird in her hands. She was familiar, yet different, and that intrigued him. Slightly reserved at times, definitely opinionated, quick to laugh, though. She'd always had a gift for working with animals, but it was more refined now; her confidence, skill and intelligence were clearly evident as she moved among herds of cattle that could flatten her with a swish of a tail.

Watching this sexy, five-foot-three dynamo walk right up to an unpredictable cow and sweet-talk it into submission was quite a sight.

As he stood there holding the birdcage, ignoring the bee buzzing around his hat, Sunny lifted her head and looked right at him. He could have sworn the air arced with electricity.

They were going to have to do something about that. Otherwise all these sparks would likely set off a brushfire the size of Texas.

The problem was, he already had one potential disaster on his hands. Inviting another was sheer lunacy.

What he *did* need to do was talk to his daughter. Soon. Tori had already been abandoned once—and three years later, she still hadn't fully recovered. Overnight, it seemed, she'd gone from a precocious, energetic, happily rambunctious six-year-old to a poster child for manners, good behavior and decorum.

Hell, most people would say he had the perfect kid. But it just wasn't right. He'd seen the unguarded side of her, and it tore him up that he hadn't been able to coax that part of her back out.

But Sunny had—or was making progress, at least.

He didn't want to cause a setback, but he had to make sure Tori understood that Sunny wouldn't be here forever.

He wouldn't have the little girl he'd watched come

into this world build false hopes that would only break her heart.

As for his heart—what did it matter? It was already beyond repair.

Had been for ten long years.

Chapter Twelve

Sunny was out of the house before daylight the next morning, her mind racing, but getting her absolutely nowhere. The knots in her stomach were almost squeezing the life out of her, and impatience was riding her hard.

So far she hadn't accomplished a thing. She felt scattered, edgy, and didn't have any answers—about the dead cows or Jackson Slade.

How in the world had she convinced herself she could see him again—live in his house, for crying out loud—and not trip herself up with emotions?

In the cool interior of the barn, she turned on the lights and checked on the parrot, then unlatched Violet's stall and slipped in to have a look at the mare and foal. She spent several indulgent moments petting the baby horse. Then she took a moment to gaze around.

Each stall had an opening that led to sectioned-off paddocks so the horses had plenty of room to roam. The changes Jack had made on the ranch in only three years were impressive. Facilities that had once been sagging from neglect now showed the pride of hard work and caring. And despite the constant activity normal for a highly successful spread, it was peaceful.

She sighed and dropped a kiss on Beauty's nose. Like her dam, the foal had a sweet disposition. And like a typical youngster, she wasn't shy about seeking attention.

"You're going to make your future veterinarian's job very easy because you're so sociable," Sunny crooned, feeling a pang that it wouldn't be her. After treating Violet to a good scratch, she wiped her hands on the seat of her jeans and left the stall.

Needing to do something productive, she sat down on a wooden bench in the stables and plucked her cell phone out of her pocket. Marty's private line was programmed on her speed dial, so she punched it in and listened to the ten rapid tones she could probably hum from memory if she had an ounce of musical talent. Which she didn't—much to her mother's embarrassment. After Sunny had delivered an impromptu solo in church—she'd gotten carried away and belted out the first three lines of a hymn's final verse before she realized no one else was still singing—Anna had instructed her to never, ever sing again in church.

Marty's line wasn't engaging, so she disconnected and hit speed dial again. It rang this time, just as she happened to glance through the open door of the barn. The sky had lightened, but the sun wasn't yet over the horizon.

"Oh, crud. I forgot about the time difference again," she muttered. Before she could quickly hit the End button, Marty answered.

"I hope you realize you're a pain in the south end of a chicken going north," he said.

Sunny thought about that for a minute. "Maybe I'm

not yet awake. Is that one of your riddles, or do you have a headache? And how'd you know it was me?''

''Caller ID. I've got a doozy of a headache, thanks for asking. And if the south end of the chicken is headed north, which part of those tail feathers don't you understand?''

She grinned. ''Okay, okay. I'm a pain in your head *and* your butt. Sounds like you haven't had your coffee yet. Want me to call back when you're more civil?''

''I never *stopped* drinking coffee, babe.''

''You've been there all night?''

''Yeah, a certain little blonde keeps badgering me with phone calls and I'm forced to work all night. I only do this for women I really love, you know.''

''I'll keep you stocked in jelly beans for life.''

''That's what I like to hear. You, on the other hand, may or may not like to hear my news.''

Her hand tightened on the receiver, and the knots in her stomach twisted a millimeter tighter. ''I'm about as tough as they come. Lay it on me.''

''I'm only a quarter of the way through with the herd serum. We got in a local case of *C. botulinum* and this place is hopping, so—''

''Was it contracted through soil spores or feed?'' The interruption was automatic and innate.

''Feed. Lots of little chicken organisms in it. Way too many for the producer to plead ignorance.''

Which meant, Sunny knew, that someone would likely be prosecuted.

''Anyway, babe, you don't need to get tangled up in what's going on here, too. Which is why I got behind on your case. It's a little tough to tell the boss I'm busy with a cooler full of cow blood from our esteemed Dr. Carmichael, when said doctor's supposed to be vacationing.''

"Don't get yourself in trouble, Marty. I mean it. If something comes up, you direct it to me, you hear?''

"I hear you, babe, but I've still got your back covered.''

Marty was such a sweetheart. He made her laugh, was a loyal friend and rated much better than average in the looks department. Why couldn't she have fallen for him?

Because she was an idiot, that was why.

She was still hung up on a sexy cowboy who sported a diamond stud in his left ear and wore a tobacco-colored Stetson that made her weak in the knees when he tugged it down just so. A cowboy who did for a pair of chaps what Baryshnikov did for a pair of tights—made you drool.

And the worst part of it was there were no second chances for them. What they'd had together ten years ago didn't mesh with who they were today. Oh, she could have an affair with him, but more than that just wasn't in the cards. He had a seven-day-a-week commitment to his Texas ranch, and she had twelve-hour days waiting for her in California.

And dwelling on that wasn't doing her a bit of good.

"So, what have you found out about my cows, Marty?''

"Zip. That's the good news. So far, all the ones I've tested come up healthy as cows in clover.''

"I think that's *happy* as cows in clover. What about the specimens from the expired Angus?''

"I'm still working on that. I've tried getting a positive on every disease remotely relative to the information you gave me from your field observation, and every test turns up nonreactive. That's the rest of the good news. The bad news is you've still got dead cows and no explanation or diagnosis. But I'm not giving up just yet.''

That wasn't good. ''Why?''

''Something doesn't feel right. Or maybe I've just been hanging around you too long and you're turning me into a Worry Willy. I want to try a couple of different techniques.''

The knot in her stomach clenched tighter. Special testing was expensive and time-consuming. Sometimes it could take months to complete. And Marty wasn't the type to waste money or time on a whim.

''What is it you're looking for?''

''Give me some time, babe.''

She stood up and paced the length of the barn. She couldn't tell if that nonanswer was an evasion or merely a distraction. Marty's attention span was pretty much hit and miss when he had sophisticated lab toys at his fingertips.

''I don't have a lot to spare. I can only stay in Texas until the end of the month. That's two weeks away.''

''I hear you, and I'm on it. Now, quit talking to me and hang up, so I can go drink another gallon of caffeine and get to work. And while I'm at it, I think I'll fax you the definition of *vacation*. That's supposed to be what you're on, you know, spending a little time to recharge your batteries.''

''My batteries are being charged just fine.'' Overcharged, if she wanted to be truthful about it. ''And remember what I said. Don't take any heat for me.''

''I'm hanging up, Doc.''

''Just one more thing.'' She heard the heavy sigh that didn't quite mask the chuckle. ''Thank you,

Marty. I mean that. I really appreciate what you're doing.''

''Just send jelly beans.''

She shook her head and smiled as the dial tone buzzed in her ear. Marty would go to bat for her in an instant.

But that wasn't going to be necessary. One way or another, those supplies she'd requisitioned would be accounted for.

If it turned out they were just barking in the dark, she'd be handing Jack a bill. He'd gladly pay it, too, since it would make a small dent in his wallet compared with having his entire herd destroyed.

The other means of accountability, of course, would be the filing of an official health-hazard report—in which case the supplies would be justified and the beef operation Jack had worked so hard to build would be in grave jeopardy.

She hoped to God it was the former. But Marty's tenacity regarding the primary specimen sent a chill of foreboding up her spine.

When she turned around, she jumped, sucking in air so hard she nearly choked.

Jack stood three paces behind her, holding two steaming mugs of coffee. She slapped a palm to her chest where her heart was doing a fine imitation of a wild stallion's gallop.

''You ought to have the decency to make a little noise. You scared the daylights out of me.''

''Sorry. I didn't want to interrupt.'' He held out a mug. ''Beau said you're supposed to drink this, then get your skinny bones inside and eat breakfast.''

''My bones aren't skinny.'' The aroma of coffee made her stomach growl. She took a sip and nearly moaned. Beau was an absolute master in the kitchen. "And I don't believe he said that."

"Exact words—except he didn't say 'bones.'"

Since his gaze dipped tellingly to her hips, she could easily fill in the word. "That part of me's not skinny, either. And what's with men insulting my backside, anyway? That's twice now, and the sun's hardly up."

He took a sip of his own coffee, watching her over the rim of the cup. "Another man insulted you? Tell me who and I'll go beat him up."

"Oh, no. That'll never do. Marty's a nice guy."

"How nice?"

Jack was clearly fishing. Although his tone was easy—pleasant, even—his eyes narrowed just enough to give him away. "Friend nice," she said, meeting his gaze head-on. "Satisfied?"

"Not hardly."

The words were barely above a whisper, yet they slammed into her like a butting goat, stealing her breath. He'd just put her on notice…very effectively.

"You want to go have some breakfast while you fill me in on that phone call? I heard enough of the conversation to know you don't have an answer, but I'd like to hear the details."

"I'm not really hungry." Not for food. And she didn't want to chance everyone in the household glimpsing the arousal she was sure blazed across her face like neon at an exotic dance club.

"Beau figured you'd say that, so he sent me with this." Jack leaned down and picked up a bag he'd set on the bench, the clear, sealed plastic fogged with steam.

Sunny's stomach growled. "Are those fresh muffins?"

"Yes. But I have to warn you. Beau's been experimenting again, and he claims these are loaded with healthy energy stuff."

She accepted the muffin he held out. "Did you try one?"

"Yeah. They're pretty good."

Obviously, since he'd brought one for himself, as well. She bit into the warm muffin. "Oh, they're fabulous. Banana? What else is in this?"

"I have no idea. That's why I felt it'd be gentlemanly to offer a disclaimer—in case he slipped an aphrodisiac in there and you end up with extra energy and insist on having your way with me."

She stared at him, her mouth open, the muffin suspended in her hand. He was reaching into the plastic bag, as though getting a rise out of her hadn't even occurred to him.

That was the second blatantly suggestive remark he'd made this morning.

"Didn't you say you'd already had one of these?" she asked.

"Right out of the oven."

"Then maybe you shouldn't eat another one."

He laughed deeply and unrestrainedly, startling the horses. They all came to hang their heads over the stall doors to see what the commotion was about.

And Jack's laughter definitely caused a commotion with Sunny. He didn't laugh nearly often enough. To hear him let go, if only for a moment, made her heart soften.

"You can go ahead and eat that, sugar bear. Cora's the one who badgered Beau into learning about herbs and their uses. She wouldn't let him fool around with aphrodisiacs."

"Perhaps, but Cora's not yet here this morning, so he's got no one to monitor what he tosses into the batter. And don't be so sure of Cora's innocence. The way those two spark off each other, it's a wonder you haven't caught them naked on the kitchen table."

His brows shot up. Then a slow grin spread over his face. "You think my housekeeper and number-one cowboy are having sex?"

"I think your number-one cowboy has unofficially traded in his Stetson for a chef's hat. And I don't think they're having sex. Yet."

"You're probably right. Too much tension. Kind of like with us."

What in the world had gotten into him this morning? And why the heck wasn't she jumping at the opportunity? She'd nearly driven herself crazy imagining them making love for the remainder of the time she was here.

As a young man, Jack had been ultramasculine, hot-tempered and broody, the kind of guy who exuded the promise of sexual satisfaction with merely the intensity of his blue-eyed stare. One look and the word that came to mind was *danger*. A challenge to any girl with enough spunk to tame him.

Now that Jack was a mature man, the rough edges had rounded—due in part, she suspected, to fatherhood and success. He didn't have that mad-at-the-world chip on his shoulder that caused closed-minded gossips to speculate on how many lethal weapons he likely carried.

But he wore unquestionable confidence like the tailored fit of a fine shirt. He was a true leader, a larger-than-life presence whom others looked to for advice and guidance, even people who'd snubbed him years ago. He'd earned their respect and returned it without holding a grudge.

He was still ultramasculine, still radiated enough pheromones to sweep a woman off her feet and have her thanking him in advance because she'd be too sated to remember afterward.

And he was still thrillingly dangerous. Which suddenly, despite her bold fantasies about vacation sex, made Sunny a nervous wreck.

She realized she was staring at him like a dumbfounded maiden who'd never been flirted with before. Deliberately, she raised the muffin and took a bite.

Amusement flared in his eyes and he gave her hair a playful tug. "Come sit over here and tell me what Marty had to say."

She followed him to the bench she'd been sitting on earlier. "Are you sure there'll be enough room for the two of us and that overconfident ego of yours, as well?"

He snagged her hand and tugged. She nearly landed in his lap. That was what she got for trying to best him.

She realized that their banter had its roots in worry, was a distraction to mask their fears of 'what if.'

"So far, your herd's healthy."

"And?"

"And Marty doesn't know what killed your cow."

He swore, leaned forward and propped his elbows on his knees, then dropped his forehead into his palms. "Damn it. I'm losing money by the day. I should have loaded and shipped two railcars of beef by now. I've got buyers breathing down my neck, and I sure as hell can't tell them I've got dead livestock that may or may not have contaminated my herd."

Laying her hand against his back was instinctive. Sunny shared his frustration. "I know, Jack."

His head whipped around, his gaze spearing hers. "Do you? I don't see *your* bank account on the line here. You're the one holding the hatchet."

Her temper ignited, even as the unfair accusation tore at her insides like a razor. She shot up off the bench and faced him with fire in her eyes.

"You just hold on a damn minute. I risked my job and my license under false pretenses to keep this quiet, to make *your* life easier, and you don't show one ounce of appreciation. You could have had state *and* federal agencies crawling all over this place, spotlighting the whole town on the nightly news. Do you think it's easy for one person, *me*—" she thumbed her chest "—to handle a herd this size?"

She was so furious she could hardly see straight. "I'm *supposed* to be on a damn vacation." She marched out the barn door, then turned around and marched back in.

Lifting her chin, daring him to make a peep, she snapped, "I'm going to town." She would drag Donetta out of bed if she had to. She was in the mood for some serious male bashing. "I have my cell phone with me. If you can't recollect the number, call my mother."

With that, she whirled and headed for the Suburban, muttering the whole time. Darn it, even her dog wasn't here to support her. He was still upstairs asleep with Tori and the cat.

She was twenty feet from her truck when a masculine arm wrapped around her middle and her feet left the ground.

Instincts had her struggling as Jack wound both

arms around her waist and held her snug against his chest, her feet still dangling. She could have kicked him in the shins, but when he pressed his cheek close to her ear, she only wanted to weep.

"I'm sorry," he said.

Oh, he *would* have to use that tone, the one that was raw with sincerity and genuine remorse. The fight drained out of her. "I'm on your side, you know."

"I know. I'm an idiot." He kissed her hair, settled his cheek on hers.

"Well, no, you're not exactly an idiot. But you really, really made me mad." She felt the muscles of his face shift. "Are you smiling, Slade?"

"Yeah. Thanks for telling me where you were going."

She wasn't about to admit that it was the mature thing to do, that she'd done it for him, that the minute she'd left the barn a blinding flash from the past had spun her around like a hotel revolving door. She took a breath, aware of his forearm beneath her breasts.

"I only did it for the animals—in case they needed me."

"Um-hmm. Am I forgiven?"

She tried not to smile. "I suppose. Now would you put me down? I'm a respectable veterinarian and you're tarnishing my reputation."

"Oh, no, sugar bear. When I get around to tarnishing your reputation, you'll know it."

Her feet touched the ground. That they even held her was a wonder. Before she could fully assess the condition of her emotions, she saw Beau standing by the corner of the barn, hands on his hips, an apron tied around his waist. He was making a good effort at appearing annoyed, and failing dismally.

"See there," she whispered to Jack.

The fool man just looked down at her and grinned.

"I walk all the way out here," Beau said, "to fetch the two of you to breakfast, and there you are, sparkin' in the middle of the yard, and the sun hasn't hardly peeped up. Ya'll better come inside before my perfectly fine breakfast goes stone-cold."

"Sorry, Beau," Jack called, "not this morning. We've got work to do." He slung an arm around Sunny's shoulders. Beau threw up his hands and stalked back toward the house—though his bowlegged gait looked more like a jig.

"I think you're wrong about him and Cora not having sex," Jack said, urging her toward the barn. "He reads foreplay into a mere settling of differences. Definitely a man with romance on his mind. And it's been a long time since I've seen him high-step it across the yard. That looked like the walk of a happy man to me."

"Romance and sex aren't the same thing—and no," Sunny said before he could interrupt, "I'm not going to spell that out for you, so don't ask. And I stand by my original opinion. They haven't done it because he's still talking about it. That says frustration, loud and clear."

"Sounds a lot like us."

"I guess it does."

The stumble was barely noticeable, his tone utterly casual. "Want to do something about it?"

"Not right now, thanks."

"Just checking."

She ducked her head and smiled. "That's allowed. Where are we going, by the way?"

"To saddle the horses. I figured we'd have a look around, see what kind of trouble we run into."

"I'd just as soon stay out of trouble, if it's all the same to you."

He chuckled, dropped a kiss on her temple and headed toward the tack room, presumably to get saddles.

Her heart thudded, and for a minute she felt disoriented. Something had shifted between them. She didn't know how to define it, exactly. It just felt... more at ease, natural.

She'd already brushed and haltered a bay gelding and was leading it out of the stall when she heard the echo of Jack's boot against concrete.

The sight of him walking down the center aisle of the barn, carrying two saddles as though they were mere blankets, had her halting in her tracks. Somebody ought to capture that masculine sensuality on film, she thought. Transplant the man to California and he'd be in a movie pronto.

The gelding nudged her in the back, snapping her out of her trance. She took a breath and waited for Jack to set down the saddles.

"You get to do the honors," she said, holding out the reins.

His brows lifted. "This isn't my mount."

She grabbed his hand, slapped the reins in his palm and walked back to the stall. "It's nice to see you're on the ball this morning. By the time you get mine rigged out, I'll have brought yours here."

"Now, that's a pure-and-simple female thing. What happened to the I-can-do-anything-you-can-do woman?"

She glanced at him over the stall door, noted he

already had the pad and saddle in place, and gave him a cheeky grin. "Oh, she's still around."

He snorted and tightened the cinch. "Are you flirting with me, Sunny Leigh?"

She led his roan out and handed him the reins, relieving him of the ones he held. "You think a woman's flirting when she asks you to saddle her horse?"

"When it's you asking, I do."

She smiled and walked her horse out of the barn. She was waiting at the end of the fence when he rode up next to her. Their legs practically brushed, and she had to scramble to keep the bay steady.

"You forgot something." He plucked her hat from his saddle horn and shoved it on her head. "We need to get you a new one. That pitiful excuse for a cowboy hat has dog's teeth marks in it."

She adjusted the brim, made sure the crown wasn't smashed. "Don't pick on my hat. It happens to be my favorite one."

"Guess there's no accounting for taste." His lips quirked, and he urged his horse forward.

Sunny ignored his remark. It was a cute hat.

She caught up with him, and they rode out across the pastures, eyes peeled for any livestock acting sick or abnormal. Jack stopped a couple of times to check fences, and when they finally circled back to the creek, it was close to noon, the sun baking the earth and Sunny's arms, as well.

"You want to stop and rest?" he asked, riding up next to her.

"My tailbone would appreciate it. I don't get to ride often at home."

She dismounted beneath the shade of a cottonwood.

She wasn't sure how he had managed it, but he was already on the ground and right there to help her, his hands steadying her waist until her feet touched the ground.

"Thanks." Although the aid had been unnecessary, the gallantry charmed her. She'd noticed that he'd grown quieter as they'd ridden. This ranch was beautiful and impressive. As he'd surveyed his land, she knew this sense of waiting for the other boot to fall was getting to him. Their argument this morning was a prime example.

And she was just as antsy as he was, because she didn't yet have any answers.

But she *did* have a suspicion that was growing stronger by the day.

"Jack, do you have any enemies?"

He frowned and tugged off his leather gloves. "I suppose I could. But I can't name any off-hand. Why?"

"Because something just doesn't feel right to me. It's like I'm looking in the wrong direction. My initial thought was that your cows must have just lain down and died peacefully. I considered cardiac arrest, but the age isn't consistent with that possibility and I doubt you'd have two animals die that close together from the same heart disorder. I did note a couple of postmortem signs that could indicate disease, but when the lab tests ruled them out, I started to wonder if my mother's urgency over the phone had colored my judgment. If I'd read more into this than was warranted because I was *expecting* to encounter disaster."

"It's not like you to second-guess yourself."

"I was speaking in the past tense." Water burbled over smooth stones in the creek, tempting her to kick off her boots and wade. "I'm just not used to running up against a brick wall."

"I don't see how any of this relates to enemies."

"It doesn't. But poison would. And the foamy saliva would corroborate it."

"Poison would show up in the lab test, Sunny."

"Normally, yes. But the nonreactive results are nagging at me. I'm missing something, and I keep coming back to that. Plus Marty's doing some more extensive, specialized testing, which tells me he's worried. And when Marty worries, I get really edgy."

"So what's next?"

"I think you should station guards over your herd, assign your men around-the-clock shifts. I realize it's a lot to ask of them on top of their other duties. If you're short on manpower, I'll take a shift, too."

"Like hell. If you think somebody's messing with my livestock, there's no way I'll let you put yourself in the middle of an ambush."

"I know how to defend myself, and I know how to shoot a gun—and hit what I'm aiming at!"

"No one's questioning your marksmanship. But my answer's still no."

"I don't recall asking a question." She had defense skills that went beyond marksmanship, but the way he was scowling at her, she decided to keep that to herself.

"I'll assign guards because I trust your opinion. But *you* won't be one of them."

She shrugged, letting him have the last word. She'd gotten her way, and—although his tone could have used a little sugar—a compliment to boot.

Chapter Thirteen

Sunny stood on the porch and wrapped her arm around the post, enjoying the country night. She'd showered and changed into a short summer dress that skimmed her body and made her feel feminine.

Fireflies blinked in the dark as a choir of insects sang their hearts out. A warm breeze stirred the air, carrying with it the sultry perfume of jasmine from the garden a few feet away. When the front door opened, she glanced back and smiled as Jack stepped outside.

"I can't get over Tori going home with your mom like she did," he said, joining her at the rail.

Anna Carmichael had stopped by earlier with an apple pie, and Beau had flattered her into staying for supper. Somewhere between the pot roast and the pie à la mode, Anna had decided Tori should come help her make angel cookies for the seniors at the retirement center. Jack had nearly fallen out of his chair when Tori asked if she could go.

"Mama's dying to brush up on her grandmother skills, hoping that me or Storm will take the hint and provide her some."

"Do you plan to?"

"Someday. When the time's right." A coyote

yipped in the distance, and she wondered if the animal would catch a rabbit and be satisfied rather than stalk someone's livestock.

"It's so beautiful here," she said quietly. "Leaving must have been difficult for you."

"I didn't have much choice. My dad had nearly run the ranch into the ground—I never understood how he managed to keep the taxes and mortgage paid up on a place this size. But that's about all he did, besides drink. He knew I wanted to do something with the land, and out of spite, or pure meanness, he refused to turn the ranch over to me. He pointed a shotgun at me when I tried to slap a coat of paint on the barn. That pretty much cinched it."

"I'm sure it was the alcohol that made him treat you that way."

He shrugged. "Lanette wanted out of this town, so we went to Dallas and I got a job working at an insurance agency."

Sunny nearly choked. "Holy crud! Insurance? As in, desk job? Didn't it smother you?"

Jack grinned. Sunny would know that about him—that he wouldn't be happy cooped up in an office. Lanette hadn't cared.

"Nearly. I quit after a few months and signed on to work for a big cattle outfit outside of Dallas. Learned as much as I could, things my dad didn't know or hadn't bothered to teach me. I saved every spare dollar and made some good investments—which paid off when it came time to fix up this place."

"Were you surprised when your dad left you the ranch?"

"Very. It was all I'd ever wanted. Linc has a share in it, too, but he's never claimed it, wouldn't even come home for the funeral. I couldn't blame him. Linc always got the brunt of Dad's drunken rages.''

Jack gazed up at the inky sky, which formed a canopy over his land. Pride filled his chest, as it always did where this ranch was concerned. The animals were settled for the night, and the lights were off in the bunkhouse. The men who weren't out watching over the herd would grab every minute of sleep before their shift came.

His soul was in this land, in this house.

He didn't like the worry and suspicion that threatened his peace and everything he'd worked so hard for.

"I didn't think twice about coming home," he continued. "Dad was gone, and that gave me the freedom to do things my way. What I'd inherited was pretty much a few broken-down structures and a vast expanse of brown and dying grass, with a few underfed steers tossed in for decoration. But I had a picture in my mind of exactly how this place could be, and I worked eighteen hours a day to get it there. Lanette wasn't happy about being back in Hope Valley, though, especially when she got a look at the ranch.''

He shrugged, leaned his shoulder against the post. "So she left.''

"I'm sorry.''

"No need. I'd kept my part of the bargain.'' He'd shouldered his responsibilities. Numbed his emotions and locked them away where they couldn't haunt and destroy him. He hadn't loved Lanette, but he'd been a good husband. Only with Tori had he dared to unlock his heart and soul. Remembering how he'd felt when he'd first laid eyes on that tiny baby brought a lump to his throat. "It was Lanette's choice to leave and send divorce papers."

"Was Tori with Lanette when she died?"

"No. Tori was with me. The last time they saw each other was the day Lanette walked out."

"Oh. I thought…" Sunny shook her head. "Never mind."

"No, finish what you were going to say."

"Obviously, I don't know the whole story. I wondered about Tori's tendency to withdraw, thought maybe she'd been traumatized by her mother's death."

"She was six when Lanette split. That was traumatic enough. I shouldn't complain. She's a perfect kid. Just…too perfect sometimes."

"She's doing better lately."

"Yeah. I caught her dancing through the house with one of the chickens."

"A real one?"

"Feathers and all. She was singing at the top of her lungs about some purple monster." He smiled at the memory, settled his gaze on Sunny. Her blond hair was a riot of soft curls, and tended to bush out in balmy weather. She hated it, he knew, but that tousled, sexy look inspired red-hot fantasies in any man with a set of eyes and a drop of testosterone in his blood.

She looked young and fresh, her face free of makeup except for the sheen of gloss on her lips. Her silky slip of a dress, held in place with skinny straps he could probably snap with one finger, displayed unblemished skin kissed golden by the sun. Part California tan and part Texas.

Her world…and his. Panic chilled his heart and he slammed the door on the part of his soul that wanted to howl at the injustice of fate. They were talking about Tori.

"The child running through the house with my best laying hen is a far cry from the girl who normally takes great care to scrub her hands so she won't leave dirt smudges on the towels," he said. "It's because of you, you know."

"Now, don't go blaming me for chicken feathers in the house." Sunny's green eyes tilted up at the corners. "I'll plead the Fifth Amendment on the dirty towels, though."

He chuckled, because he was guilty of ruining a few towels himself. "She can bring every single one of the hens into the living room if she wants. She's finally being a...a girl. I've racked my brain for the past three years, trying to get inside her head, get her to loosen up. You did it in less than a week."

He didn't want to spoil the evening, but Tori wasn't home and he needed to address the issue of his daughter's fragile feelings. He rested his palm on Sunny's shoulder, slid it down her arm and took her hand.

"I don't want you to take this the wrong way, Sunny, but I don't want to see my daughter get hurt."

She studied him for a long moment, then squeezed his hand, her voice a melancholy murmur against the backdrop of cicadas. "When I leave, I think you're trying to say."

"Yes." He expected her to be defensive. Instead, her eyes softened with genuine compassion.

"I wouldn't do that to her, Jack. I'm aware of the attachment she's formed, and we've talked about it. She knows I have to go back to California at the end of the month. She'll be fine."

But would he?

He should have known Sunny would be sensitive to Tori's feelings, would take every care with her well-being. Sunny was going to be a great mother one of these days.

His gut was tangled up worse than a calf in barbed wire. Bringing up the subject had taken a lot out of him. Yet Sunny had surprised him, let him off easy.

How could she stand there so relaxed, so damn gorgeous, when he felt as though he was drowning in quicksand? He wondered how she would react if she knew his heart was still in her hands. She'd given it back to him ten years ago, but just as a pet animal could find its way home to loved ones against great odds, so had his heart.

She leaned her hips against the low porch rail, and he lost the entire thread of the conversation. That flirty little dress had been driving him crazy all night.

"I can't take all the credit for Tori's changes, you know. I had a little help from friends."

"Now, that scares me. I know your friends." He forced his gaze away from her short hemline. "While we're on the topic, I've been meaning to ask what went on at your mother's after Storm and I were called away to the traffic accident. That was when I really noticed the shift in Tori's behavior."

For some reason, his words brought a genuine, sassy smile to her face and impish delight to her eyes. It flat-out charmed him.

"Sorry, cowboy. My lips are sealed. Us Texas Sweethearts have a confidentiality rule."

"We're talking about my daughter here." He gave himself points for keeping a straight face—and his hands to himself.

"Uh-uh." She shook her head. "No way. Sealed tight."

When she clamped her lips together to punctuate the playful words, his body went from semihard to iron in an instant. By damn, he was about to lose the points he'd just earned.

"I bet I can unseal them."

"Better men than you have tried," she teased.

"Think so?" He crowded her against the porch rail. "You know, don't you, that that's a dare I can't refuse." With her back against the wooden post, he leaned in, slid his knee between her thighs and pressed upward.

Nice and firm.

She sucked in a breath, her eyes going wide. Pure masculine satisfaction pumped in his chest as he watched emotions flash in those expressive green eyes. Stunned…oh, yes. Aroused—absolutely. Her lips parted.

"Your mouth's open, sugar bear." Cupping her face in his hands, he bent his head and kissed her.

He realized in an instant that he'd miscalculated. One touch and all the familiar memories crashed over him like a bale of hay falling from a storage loft, scattering his feeling like straw in the wind.

What had started as a dare had gotten out of control. Lifting his head took every drop of strength he possessed.

SUNNY LOOKED UP AT JACK, her hands still clasped behind his neck. She wasn't absolutely sure she could speak, was fairly certain her lungs had malfunctioned.

She cleared her throat. "That wasn't fair. Sealed lips mean no telling."

The corner of his mouth kicked up in a half smile. "I like my interpretation better."

"So do I." She wasn't sure who made the first move, but she didn't care because his mouth was right where she wanted it. Against hers.

Years of longing collided with passion, wrenching a moan from deep in her throat. The sound of surrender whipped the power of the kiss into a raging storm faster than lightning could split the sky.

His arms wrapped around her waist and his knee wedged between her thighs, pressing, setting her on fire. She buried her fingers in his hair, held on, her mind screaming, *at last.* His taste, his scent, his skill and sexual confidence were as familiar as her own face in a mirror.

He cupped the back of her thigh, lifted, hauled her closer still, then bunched up the hem of her dress and slid his palm over her behind. When his fingertips grazed the juncture of her thighs, a kaleidoscope of brilliant colors exploded and the world seemed to fade away. Her hips bucked, seeking more, harder.

They fed on each other in a frenzy of need, restless hands tangling as they sought to touch, moans ending in impatient whimpers, bodies pressing in a desperate race to reach that promised bliss.

He jerked his head back and she dazedly gulped in air. She finally realized that the buzz inside her head was the sound of the cicadas rejoicing in the night.

Her hands slipped off his shoulders, down to his elbows. She felt his erection straining against his jeans as he held her hips firmly against him and leaned his forehead against hers.

"This isn't right." His voice was raspy, his breath hitching as though he'd run a marathon.

"Yes, it is." Confusion swirled. He had her so aroused the only sensation she could identify in her body was the throb of desire between her legs. She tightened her grip on his arms. "Don't you dare stop now."

He lifted his head, the burning intensity in his blue eyes both a warning and a promise.

"I don't intend to stop, sugar bear. I meant it's not right that we're going at it like rabid coyotes ripping into a lamb."

She eased a bit. His analogy wasn't exactly romantic, but... "It was working for me."

"Are you sure?" His gaze remained on hers.

Astonished, she felt her jaw go slack. "Of course I'm sure. Couldn't you tell?"

His lips curved. "I meant, are you sure about this? Us? I've been dead determined to get you into a motel room or my bed ever since we started this dance. But I have to know it's what you want. I'm tied up in knots, sugar bear, and if I loosen them, I won't want to stop."

She laced her fingers behind his neck and tugged until his lips were a sigh away from hers. "I was a Girl Scout. We excel at untying knots."

Elation and surrender rumbled in his throat and flared in his eyes an instant before he covered her lips, accepting her invitation. Without breaking the kiss, he swept his arm beneath her thighs and lifted her.

"What in the world?" A breeze whispered over her naked behind. She snatched at the hem of her dress, tried to hold it in place.

"I'm going to seduce you, sugar bear. And it's not going to be out on the porch."

"Oh... Well."

He paused, frowned. "What's that digging into my side?"

She thought for a minute. "My cell phone. My dress doesn't have pockets. I clipped it to my panties."

"I can't wait to see how you managed that on a G-string. Or how the hell I missed it."

"It's tiny. No sense in gouging you, though. Why don't you put me down and I'll walk—or run. It'll be faster."

"Sugar bear, I swore when I got you in my arms that I wasn't letting you go."

He had that determined look on his face that told her he had his own agenda and she should save her breath. He navigated the door, kicked it closed and twisted the dead bolt, but Sunny couldn't fully appreciate his skill because she was still busy grabbing for her elusive hem.

She had no idea where this sudden modesty came from, couldn't bring herself to actually admit it. But it made her feel out of control.

"Relax, sugar."

That was like asking Simba to squeeze through a mouse hole. Impossible.

Desire still simmered, but unaccountable nerves hummed beneath her skin, fluttered in her stomach like butterfly kisses. She wanted this night to be perfect. Yet she was suddenly as jumpy as a spinster virgin.

He was a man in a hurry to get them to the bedroom, and she grabbed his shoulders, self-preservation winning out over modesty. But when he turned the corner and mounted the stairs two at a time her brain scrambled.

Holy crud! Her bare behind had just winked at her in the hall mirror like a giant peach.

"No sense tugging at that dress. I'll have it off of you in a minute."

"In the meantime I'm mooning whoever happens to come into the living room!" The spindled wooden banister ran the length of the stairs, then continued around the corner, guarding the edge of the hallway to ensure safety, yet open so that the second floor was visible from the living room below.

His lips twitched, but he paused at the top of the stairs, used his knee to support her weight and smoothed the hem over her curves, anchoring it with his arm.

And then he kissed her. A kiss that soothed and aroused, blanked her mind of everything but that very moment.

"No one's here—except Beau," he said softly as he continued down the hall. "And he's clear over in the other wing of the house. Once he takes out his hearing aids, he wouldn't hear a stick of dynamite if it went off right beside his bed."

Sunny rested her head against Jack's shoulder and sighed. "I hate to admit this, but I think I'm scared."

They were in his bedroom now, the lamp on the nightstand switched on low. He lowered her feet to the floor, ran his hands up her arms to her shoulders, tenderly framed her face in his palms and tipped it up to his.

"Me, too, Sunny."

The admission, and the gentle touch of his lips, steadied her. She'd never known another man who could kiss as seductively as Jack.

He didn't try to swallow her whole. He simply enjoyed the process, slowly building the fires of passion, absolutely sure of where he intended to go.

She'd been prepared for wild, physically demanding sex—the way she remembered it being between them, the way they'd begun on the porch. She hadn't expected this tender assault on her emotions, this heart-pounding, unfamiliar sense of being cherished.

It frightened her. She was honest enough to admit that ten years of trying to smother her feelings for Jack, tamping down embers that only needed air to be fanned into flames, hadn't worked. She'd promised herself she could handle it—as long as she held back at least a small part of herself.

He was sabotaging her efforts, though. With tenderness. Toying and nibbling, bestowing a hundred incredible kisses that seemed to blend into one.

She reached up and encircled his wrists, needing to touch. But he took her hands and held them down at her sides, his fingertips trailing back up her arms. He slipped one spaghetti strap of her dress off a shoulder, then the other. She tipped her head to the side as he kissed his way over her cheek and down her neck.

"You smell good. Like cinnamon candy. I've dreamed about that scent."

His mouth feasted as though she tasted the same way. Arousal clenched inside her.

"Jack." Part murmur, part moan, his name was all she could manage. She wanted to tell him to hurry up, but her mind fogged, filled with too many tactile sensations for her to form coherent speech.

He reached behind her and lowered her zipper, his fingertips a slow caress down her spine as he smoothed the silky slip dress over her curves and then let it fall on the floor. The dress didn't allow for a bra, and a draft cooled by the air conditioner whispered over her bare skin and pebbled her nipples.

"I don't think you'll be needing this." He unhooked the tiny cell phone from the elastic band at the side of her panties, then set it on the nightstand.

Then he stepped back and looked at her. His eyes never wavering, he unbuttoned his shirt and shrugged it off.

His body was perfect, honed by hard physical labor rather than by working out at a gym. His gaze was like a caress. Every atom of her being hummed as her eyes catalogued each masculine detail of the man standing two feet away—familiar details, and the ones altered by time.

When his hands went to the snap of his jeans, she stepped forward. "Let me."

He hesitated, and she wondered if they were going to butt heads over control. She was counting on a fifty-fifty split in that department. The clock on the nightstand ticked, drawing attention to the silence.

A vein pulsed at his temple and his hands dropped to his sides.

Still his gaze didn't waver.

She slid her left hand inside his waistband, felt the muscles of his stomach contract as her fingers grazed his abdomen, then moved downward…and encountered the velvety, moist tip of his erection.

"No skivvies." She'd intended the comment to be boldly teasing, but her voice trembled.

Heart pumping, she closed her left palm around the tip of him, squeezed gently, then slid her hand all the way down, as the fingers of her other hand flicked open metal buttons. He sucked in a sharp breath, the sound filling her with feminine power.

His jeans now open, she cupped both hands around him and reversed the path, felt the steely, hot beat of his pulse against her palms as she inched her way back to the tip. Wanting to see and touch all of him, she grasped the denim waistband.

His hands shot out and clasped her wrists.

She glanced up at him, whispered, ''You're still a little overdressed.''

He raised her hands to his lips and kissed her palms, sending a jolt of pleasure straight to her core.

''I've got plans for you, sugar bear, and none of them includes racing out of the barn before the gate's open. Which is likely to happen if you keep touching me that way.''

She might have argued over the issue of control, but he didn't give her the chance. He kissed her neck, the swell of her breast, distracted her when his mouth closed over her nipple, his clever tongue sending pure bliss sizzling from the roots of her hair to her toes.

It had been so long. No man had ever brought this intensity of pleasure, never taken her so far, so fast.

Only Jack.

Her head fell back and her eyes closed. His palms stroked her body, gently squeezed her behind, slid between her legs, his fingertips circling, teasing. Need coiled in her belly. She was hardly aware that he'd slipped off her panties and laid her on the bed until the cool sheets met her overheated skin.

When she opened her eyes, he'd kicked off his jeans and was easing on top of her. She cradled him between her thighs, desperation and need colliding. Heels digging into the mattress, she raised her hips, an invitation, a demand.

But instead of thrusting, he lifted his body off her, shifting so they had plenty of room in the bed.

"Uh-uh," he murmured. "I've barely gotten started."

She grabbed the sheet in her fist, nearly screamed. "Well, I'm way ahead of you, cowboy, so you better catch up."

His smile grew wider. "I like my position just fine. Feel free to cross the finish line without me—as many times as you like." He trailed his fingers around the healing abrasion on her thigh. "I'll keep up. In fact, I'll do my best to help you out...as many times as you want."

"What if I only want the main one?"

He shook his head. Tsked. "I bet you still read the last page of a novel first."

"I like to know what's coming, so I can relax and enjoy the story."

His fingers stilled. His gaze snapped to hers. "You know what's coming, sugar bear. And it'll be both of us. So relax and enjoy. I'll take care of the surprises."

His sensual self-assurance was a thrilling aphrodisiac—because she knew for a fact he could deliver.

But relaxing was not an option. The instant his lips touched her skin, tension snapped in her veins like live wires arcing against metal.

He kissed the bruise on the side of her knee, then the one on her shin. He sought out every slight contusion and ministered to it with the utmost, tender care.

It was the most heart-stopping, erotic thing she'd ever experienced.

He knew exactly where to stroke to bring a gasp, the right amount of pressure to exert to make her writhe and cry out. As though determined to uphold a sacred vow, he took his time, lingered, toyed, aroused.

With his lips and his hands, he sent her spiraling into what felt like an endless climax, again and again.

"No more," she finally said when she could form the words. "I need you inside me. Now, Jack."

This time he didn't hesitate. She was ready. More than ready. She raised her knees, felt the tip of him press against her, enter, then stop. She whimpered, her body pulsing hard, squeezing the head of his penis.

"Give me a minute, sweetheart."

Although her body still throbbed, she went still. He usually called her sugar, or sugar bear. The only times he'd ever called her sweetheart was the night he'd told her he loved her and the day she'd nearly drowned when she'd hit her head on a tree limb while jumping into the lake.

Two, highly emotional moments. Both had filled her with joy then, and this one did now. She doubted he even realized it.

He framed her face with his hands, kissed her as though she was his world, and eased inside her all the way.

"Yes," she whispered, hooking her arms beneath his, clutching his shoulder blades. She arched and ground against him, her body relearning his. "Now."

He thrust into her deeper and harder, momentum building faster and faster. She screamed when the first climax slammed into her, and when the second one crested, he kissed her, swallowing her cries of ecstasy, trading them for his own as he surrendered and poured out his release.

Chapter Fourteen

Jack didn't have any desire to sleep. He had Sunny in his arms, and he didn't want to miss a minute of the time they had left.

He stroked his fingers up and down her arm as he held her against his side. She'd gone quiet on him. He didn't doubt he'd satisfied her. But the silence made him nervous.

"You asleep?" he asked.

"No. I'm just..." Her warm breath sighed against his chest. "I haven't been made love to like that in a very long while."

He glanced down at her. In bed after lovemaking wasn't exactly the place to bring up prior relationships, but Sunny was good at evading talk of her own life. He had her right now, and he wasn't letting go the rest of the night. So he'd satisfy his curiosity.

"I thought you were engaged."

"An engagement doesn't guarantee great sex."

Okay. He was liking this conversation. The fiancé was lousy as a lover, and she'd said Jack himself was great. Not in those exact words, but the meaning was the same.

"Is that why you called it off?"

"I didn't call it off. He dumped me."

"Guy's an idiot."

She patted his chest. "It wasn't meant to be. I think I knew that. But I haven't had the best track record with relationships. I thought I could make that one work. The kicker is, when we broke up my entire social life came to a screeching halt. People chose sides, and Michael happened to be the one with power and influence. He could get a table at Spago with only a phone call, and was on the VIP lists for all the glitzy award parties in Hollywood. I didn't have those connections."

He tightened his arm around her and squeezed. "Sounds like you had some pretty shallow friends. Do you miss going to those glitzy parties?"

"Not really. It was exciting at first. But they wouldn't let Simba come."

Jack chuckled and dropped a kiss on her head.

"Michael was…" She raised up on her elbow. "Do you really want to hear this?"

"Yeah. I really do." Like old times. Before he'd lost the right to hold her, listen to her talk.

She lay back down. "Michael was positioning himself for politics. He saw everything in terms of how much money it paid, the prestige or the opportunity to climb another rung higher up the political ladder. And he tended to sweep people along with him, expected them to do the same, want the same. He'd generate all this excitement, you know? And you'd find yourself caught up in it, thinking it was exactly what you wanted, and that it was totally your idea. That's kind of how I ended up in the job I'm in."

Her fingers idly stroked his chest. He put his hand over hers before his concentration went south.

"I'd been working at a clinic in Santa Monica and had an opportunity to buy into the business. Then Michael was having lunch with some people from the UC Davis university, and one of my former professors who happened to be there mentioned that Sam Melling—he's my boss, and most everybody in the veterinarian industry knows him—was looking to fill a top-level position and had been checking my background. Michael lives to have those kinds of opportunities dropped in his lap, and the next thing I knew I had interviews lined up and was caught up in his hype."

"You don't like your job?"

"I love my job. And I was flattered that someone like Sam Melling actually knew who I was, plus I was stunned at the deal he laid on the table. It's just…"

"Just what?"

"I don't know. It's kind of like with Mama. She's always giving me backhanded compliments. Like, 'Your hair is lovely, dear'," she mimicked, "'but you should do something with that frizz.' Or, 'Red is nice on you, dear, but you should really consider green.' I know I shouldn't buy into it, but it gets to me. Makes me feel like I'm not good enough."

"That's not so, Sun."

"You haven't dealt with her for thirty years. Michael wasn't blatant like Mama. He was more like a powerful whirlwind that I got caught up in. I found myself doing all the things he wanted me to and thinking they were my own ideas, preferences and decisions."

She pushed her hair off her face. "I'm realizing now that I've lived most of my life subconsciously trying to get Mama's unconditional approval, and I carried that pattern over to Michael. I'll be thirty next month, and it's time I stop weighing every decision against what someone else might think of it. Even coming here, the initial incentive was the opportunity to show Mama how great I am at my job. I could walk in and diagnose the problem with your herd, fix it, and she'd *see* what she's never acknowledged. That I'm damn good at what I do. Guess that pretty much flopped.''

"Don't do that, sweetheart.'' He tightened his arm around her, felt her body jolt, her heart thud against his chest. He kissed her temple. "There's not a person around who could ever doubt your skill.''

"I know,'' she said with a sigh. "I really do. Which is why I'm turning a new page in my life. I can see the flaw now, and that means I can fix it. I'm not going to let others sway my decisions and choices.'' She raised up on her elbow once more and smiled down at him, her fingers dancing softly over his chest.

"So now that I've told you about the old Sunny, what do you say to making love to the *new* one?''

He had her on top of him, his hands on her hips, rubbing her against his erection so fast she shrieked and laughed in surprise.

"If I'd known *that* was going on,'' she said, undulating against him, "I wouldn't have been boring you with my life history.''

He pulled her laughing mouth down to his. Desperately needing to be inside her, he shifted her hips and slid into where she was wet and tight—the place he wanted to stay for the rest of his life.

Panic was building in his chest. She was everything he'd always wanted in a woman. The only woman he'd ever wanted, in fact. He couldn't bear to let her go.

But he'd have to. Pleading his case, trying to change

her mind, begging her to stay wouldn't be fair. He'd lost the right to hold her ten years ago—and it had been his own fault. No, he couldn't push, not after what she'd just told him. He wouldn't manipulate her. Because if he won what his heart desperately wanted, he'd never know whether the decision was truly hers or whether she'd wake up someday and realize she'd been swept up in the powerful emotions of the moment.

He didn't want to be another one of her regrets.

So he simply made love to her. Again and again throughout the night, storing memories, guarding his heart against the inevitable.

THEY WERE STILL ASLEEP the next morning when her cell phone shrilled from the nightstand. Sunny shot up, groping in the direction of the noise, and landed on a warm masculine chest. The fog of sleep cleared in an instant, and with it came images of last night—this morning, too. Good grannie's goose. She thought she'd known all Jack's moves. He'd shown her some new ones that made her blush just thinking about them.

He reached over to the nightstand, picked up the ringing phone and handed it to her.

She accepted it, pulling the sheet up to her armpits. "Um, good morning."

His slow, sexy smile had her body throbbing with arousal. Lord, they were going to be the death of each other.

The caller ID showed Marty's private number. Sunny's mind snapped to attention.

"I'm here, Marty."

"Where's 'here,' babe? You sound half-asleep. Forget to set your alarm?"

Actually, yes. She peered at the clock, then jolted. It was already nine. Jack was usually up and out of the house before 6:00 a.m. Then again, it was doubtful they'd gotten even three hours of sleep.

"My alarm's working just fine, Marty. Do you have something for me on the test?"

"Not yet. I'm getting a reaction that suggests a toxin, but damned if I can identify it. I gotta tell you, babe, it's making me crazy."

Join the club. She wished her brain wasn't so fuzzy from lack of sleep—and marathon sex. She needed one of Beau's energy muffins.... *Energy. Herbs. Toxins.*

"Marty, what do you know about herbs? The kind that could kill a six-hundred-pound Angus?"

"I've already ruled out the toxic flora that grow in that region."

"What if the toxin wasn't ingested accidentally?" She glanced at Jack. He was sitting up with his back against the headboard. She noted the muscle working in his jaw. This couldn't be easy for him, she knew.

"What happened to that book you used to have?" she asked Marty. "The one on how to commit the perfect crime. Wasn't there something about poison herbs that don't leave incriminating traces in the blood?"

"I never got around to reading the book. I can do some research, though. It's a long shot, babe, and it'll take more time because I'll have to change the whole angle of my approach."

Her instincts told her to have him go for it. But she

was gambling with Jack's livelihood. He'd already lost too much time. "Hang on a sec."

She covered the phone with her palm and turned to Jack, repeating what Marty had told her and her own theory.

"It's your decision, Jack."

"You're saying he sees something in the test but can't link it to any cattle diseases, right?"

"Yes. We're ruling out contagious disease. But there's an organism in the specimen that reacts like a toxin. It could be genetic, in which case it'd be passed on through breeding. But my gut tells me Marty would have identified that."

"I trust your judgment, Sunny. Tell him to go ahead and do the research."

Tears stung the back of her eyes for no apparent reason. She laid her hand on his chest. "We'll give it a week. If we don't have anything by then, you can go ahead and sell your beef. But I'll find you an answer, Jack. When I get back to California, I'll keep working on it."

He picked up her hand, laced his fingers through hers. In a week she'd be gone. The bittersweet sadness in his eyes matched her own. But he understood, would let her go without a fuss. That, too, she saw in his eyes.

Lifting the phone back to her ear, she said, "Do the research, Marty," and disconnected before he could respond.

Why had she ever thought she was sophisticated enough to have vacation sex and be strong enough to walk away? Jack wouldn't stop her when the time came. It was Sunny who'd be in danger of clinging.

JACK WAS CATCHING UP on paperwork, and Sunny was at loose ends. Three days had passed since she'd made love with him. They'd mutually agreed they couldn't create an atmosphere that would send mixed signals to Tori, give her false hopes. But the look-but-don't-touch status quo was about to frazzle her nerves.

She wasn't even sure why she was still at Jack's ranch. The situation here was in limbo. But he hadn't asked her to leave, and she couldn't bring herself to make the first move. So she concentrated on keeping busy.

She'd gone to town to visit with her friends and shop at Becca's boutique. A cute little freckle-faced boy with crocodile tears in his blue eyes had stopped her on the street, Millicent Lloyd standing right behind him, and begged her to help his sick rabbit. So she'd opened the clinic and, as word spread that the vet was in town, had ended up spending six hours tending well-loved pets.

Right now she was headed toward the horse barn on the Forked S to see what Tori was up to. Sunny smiled when she saw the girl sitting in the stall, stroking the little foal, who was lying down, fast asleep, looking cute as could be.

Simba was pretending to nap, but gave himself away when he saw Sunny. His huge head popped up, ears perked, tongue hanging out, and a doggie smile played over his face. She wanted to squeeze him. She was going to miss this ranch. And Tori.

"Did you put your foal to sleep?" Sunny asked quietly, sitting down beside Tori.

"No. She was being rambunctious with Simba."

"Rambunctious, huh?" That was one of Cora's favorite words.

"Yes. And Violet got mad and made her stop. I was talking to Beauty so she wouldn't be sad because her mommy was mad at her, and she got tired and just lay down and went to sleep."

Sunny wondered if Tori was remembering a time when her own mother had gotten upset. "Animal mothers discipline their children just as people do. They want to make sure their little ones don't get hurt."

"I know. She's so cute, don't you think? I wish she could stay little like this all the time."

"Yes, baby horses are sweet." Sunny glanced at the parrot cage sitting in the corner of the stall. Tori had brought it in one day and they'd noticed that the wounded bird was calmer when he had company. Since the horses didn't seem to mind, they'd left it.

"Are you sure Beauty's not sick, Sunny?"

"Of course I'm sure. Why would you think she's sick?"

"Yesterday when she was lying down and I was petting her like this, Duane came to get saddles, and he saw Beauty and thought she was hurt or sick. I told him she was just taking a nap, but he said if anything ever happened, he'd make sure I was okay. Why did he say that if he didn't think Beauty was sick?"

"I don't know, hon. Maybe he just hasn't been around little horses that sleep so much. I promise, though. Violet and Beauty are both healthy as horses."

Tori looked up and grinned. "You're so funny."

"Yes, well this funny person needs to get some work done." She ruffled Tori's hair and raised a brow at Simba. The dog looked guilty, his brown eyes shifting to Tori, then back to her. Sunny shook her head.

"You stay here, boy." He seemed happy she'd made the decision for him.

It was just as well, because she needed to talk to Jack. She was getting that monkey-on-the-back sensation, and it usually paid to heed her intuition.

She found him in about the same position she'd seen him last, bent over the paperwork on his desk. She knocked on the open door. "Can I come in?"

He glanced up and set down his pen, closing the checkbook he'd been writing in. "Sure. What's on your mind?" His tone was casual, but his eyes were hot and hungry...and filled with a sexual frustration that matched her own.

"Same thing that's on yours, I imagine." She leaned a hip on the corner of his desk and licked her lips.

His gaze snapped to her mouth. "Where's Tori?"

"In the barn with the horses."

"Why don't you come around here and sit on my lap, then?"

"No way. I'm not starting something you can't finish. I'm not into torture."

"Damn it. We need to get a motel room."

"Make the reservations, and I'm there. In the meantime, Tori just said something that didn't sit quite right with me—"

"She was disrespectful?"

"Oh, no. Not that kind of comment. She wanted to know if I was sure Beauty wasn't sick. Evidently, Duane saw the foal lying down and told Tori he thought something was wrong. Then he told her that if anything ever happened, he'd make sure she was okay."

"Why would he think something would happen to the foal?"

"That's just it. I don't think he was talking about Beauty."

Jack frowned, clearly puzzled. "Then what?"

"I don't know. But it bothers me. How well do you really know him, Jack?"

He didn't answer for a long moment. "Are you accusing Duane of something?"

"He's been here the shortest amount of time of any of your hands. And he found both the dead cows."

"Damn it, Sunny. That's his job. The man's a friend of mine. He's not going around poisoning my cattle. That would only put him out of a job."

She slid off the desk, her stomach churning, his tone sending needles of hurt and disappointment from her heart to her toes. Maybe she was dead wrong about Duane, but for Jack to immediately jump to his friend's defense and completely dismiss her concerns pushed a hot button inside. The dismissal was like the rejection of her friends in California and her mother all over again. Always choosing sides.

"Just a thought," she said as calmly as she could manage.

"Sunny, wait. I didn't mean to snap."

"I know. And I'm probably wrong about Duane. I'm just edgy is all." She needed to get out of there before tears betrayed her. "I told Mama I'd stop by, so I better be going. You know how she is if you're five minutes late." She saw Jack start to stand, knew she'd break if he touched her. There were too many emotions swirling inside her and she couldn't seem to make sense of a single one.

"I'll be back in a while." She walked calmly out

of the office, then grabbed her keys and sprinted to the Suburban.

She hadn't actually intended to go to her mother's but ended up heading in that direction, anyway. Might as well not make a total liar out of herself. Besides, Mama always had something baking. Chocolate would be nice.

Getting so upset over Jack defending his friend was ridiculous. She'd have done the same if he'd accused Donetta of something. Besides, she was leaving in three days, anyway. She sniffed and wiped her face on her sleeve. But damn it, she was frustrated and confused, and her heart ached.

She parked under the portico of her childhood home, knocked on the front door, then went in. "Mama?"

Anna came out of the kitchen, wiping her hands on her apron. "Sunny. Are Jack and Tori with you?"

"Nope." The damn tears were threatening again. "Just me."

"Well, you're a nice surprise." They shared a warm embrace, then Anna held her at arm's length, studying her face. "You know, dear, you have such lovely features. You could do with a little makeup, though, fix yourself up a bit."

Knots twisted in Sunny's stomach as she watched her mother sit in the overstuffed chair in the living room, expecting Sunny to follow. Again she had delivered a criticism couched in a compliment.

"Right. I need to look like a fashion plate while I'm administering vaccines to a bunch of cows, and stinky tails are slapping me on the butt, leaving gooey smears of manure."

"Now, what kind of language is that for a lady?"

The censoring tone grated like fingernails on a chalkboard. Tears stung Sunny's eyes. She ought to turn around and leave, she was so close to the breaking point.

"I'm not a lady. Not in the sense you've always wanted me to be, Mama. I'm not married and keeping house, or hosting the garden club's charity auction. I've worn white shoes in the winter and velvet in the spring." Something a good Southern girl would never do. Now the tears slid down her cheeks. She was clearly in a state, but couldn't seem to rein in her emotions or her words.

"I have a career. I'm an accredited veterinarian. The government agency I happen to work for says I'm the best. I teach other vets, some of whom have been practicing since before I was even born. Why doesn't that make you proud?"

Years of built-up hurt spilled out, faster than her mother could respond.

"All my life I've tried to be who you wanted me to be, Mama, to live up to your expectations and make you proud. But no matter what, I don't measure up."

"You do."

"Then why don't you tell me? Show me?" She flicked tears from her cheek with a hand that shook. "Why do you criticize me? Why don't you love me?"

The words landed like a bomb in the silent room. Sunny's throat ached and she was shaking from head to toe. She wanted to scream, but was afraid that if she started, she'd never stop.

Her mother hadn't spoken, and Sunny looked at her, *really* looked at her. Tears rolled down Anna's face. Oh, God. Oh, my God! How could she have made her mother cry?

She dropped to her knees beside Anna's chair. "Oh, Mama. I'm sorry. I'm so sorry. I shouldn't—it's not just you. I—it's everything. I didn't mean to hurt you—"

"Shh." Anna reached out and thumbed away Sunny's tears. "I do love you, Sunny Leigh. You're my sunshine. I knew that the first time I held you in my arms."

Sunny laid her head in her mother's lap. "I know you love me. I shouldn't have said that."

"You should say what you feel. And I'm sorry if I've hurt you or criticized. I've done the best I could to be a good mother. I suppose I'm the product of how I was raised."

Anna's fingers sifted through her hair. Sunny remembered her mother doing that same thing when she was a child...when she'd been inconsolable after seeing Jack with Lanette.

Anna's gesture was a loving one. Yet Sunny had dismissed the good qualities of her mother, taken them for granted, had always been on the alert for the expected criticism.

Didn't that make her just as bad? She criticized her mother's behavior and never openly acknowledged the good.

"You used to rub my head for hours when I had a headache," she said, her cheek still on Anna's lap. "Did I ever tell you how much that meant to me?"

"There was no need to tell me, hon. When your babies grow up, you miss the times they let you hold them in your arms, cuddle them. And when your child hurts, you want to soothe her. I was filled with love and pride and purpose because I could hold you and ease your pain."

Sunny lifted her head and took her mother's hands in hers, then kissed the soft knuckles that smelled like homemade chocolate cake. "Why didn't I know that? I should have seen it. Was I so self-centered?"

"No. You've never been self-centered, Sunny. It's not in you. And you didn't know it because I was subconsciously repeating behavior I'd been taught. I just didn't realize it until today—until your tears. My own mother had a difficult life, and there were six of us children to take care of. Don't get me wrong— Grandmother Dee loved us, and we had a good family life for the most part. But she pointed out our faults, and she wasn't comfortable showing affection. Especially in public. I promised myself I wouldn't be like her when I had my own children. That I would teach them to kiss and hug. Unfortunately, the trait of criticizing followed me. But look on the bright side. When you have your children you'll be a perfect mother because you'll have the love *and* the kind disposition to go with it."

"You're kind, Mama. But that's the thing. What if I never find anyone to have children with?"

"What about Jack? He's perfect, you know, and—" Anna stopped, closed her eyes. "I'm doing it again."

Sunny patted her knee. "You do give good advice. On occasion," she added with a wink.

"Actually, it's a mother's job to give advice. Grown children don't have to take it, mind you."

"Just listen out of respect and let things go in one ear and out the other?"

Anna smiled. "That's what I did with my mother."

With her arm still on her mother's lap, she propped her chin on her fist. "What should I do, Mama?"

Anna cupped Sunny's chin and lifted her head. "About being in love with Jack?"

She nodded. "Do you have ESP, or am I that transparent?"

"Not transparent. There's much more to you than that. And I'm not just saying that because of what we discussed earlier. I'm very proud of you, Sunny Leigh. I wish you didn't live so far away, because I miss having you close by. But I understand that you've worked hard to get where you are, and I also understand how loyal Jack is to his land. Still, when the two of you are in the room together, one thing is clear. The love is blinding. I don't even think your daddy ever looked at me the way Jack Slade looks at you. It brings tears to my eyes."

"Are you sure it's not just the look of a guy who's dying to have sex?"

"Oh, that, too. As a mother, that gave me some trouble, but mark my words, hon, what's plain as day in that man's eyes goes many layers deeper than just physical wanting. It's a touching thing for a parent to realize that someone else besides you truly, truly loves your child. Knowing your child will be happy gives a parent peace."

Sunny thought about everything she and her mother had discussed. She'd run away ten years ago with a desperate need to prove herself in her mother's eyes, to be good enough that Jack would see exactly what he'd so carelessly tossed away for a cheap night of thrills. For ten years, she'd believed something was lacking in her.

"I sought the wrong goals for the wrong reasons, Mama."

"No, hon. You just took a different path, that's all.

Everything happens for a purpose. We don't always know why. Why did Daddy die? Why did Storm get shot? Why did you suffer so terribly? All I can do is speculate. I spent thirty-five of the happiest years of my life with your daddy, and I'd give up my plans to go into business in a heartbeat if I could have him back—''

''What business?''

''Oh, I hadn't meant to say anything about that yet. Wanda's selling the diner. I want to buy it.''

''Mama, that's wonderful.''

''Well, at my age some might say it's foolish. I don't have the details worked out, but we'll talk about that another time. The point is, bad things might happen, but they always set us off in a new and sometimes better direction. Storm's getting shot brought him home. I don't know where that will lead him, but at best we've reconnected. Your suffering took you to California, where you got a fine education. Now the world is wide-open to you. You have the skills to go anywhere you want with your career, choose your destiny.''

Sunny's stomach felt as though it had vaulted right up into her throat. The only thing truly stopping her from taking a chance was fear. Fear of jumping off the deep end, dumping a well-paying job and an entire lifestyle and starting over. Fear of making herself vulnerable, putting her heart fully in someone else's hands, trusting that person not to hurt her.

But darn it, if her mother had enough guts to start up a business at this stage in her life, Sunny ought to have enough courage to do the same.

She leaped up and gave Anna a smacking kiss on the cheek. "You're brilliant!"

"Where are you going?

She was already halfway out the front door. "To take another path."

Chapter Fifteen

Sunny took a shortcut on back country roads from her mother's house to Jack's ranch, her tires churning up a heavy cloud of dust on the gravel before she finally reached car-friendly asphalt. One minute she wanted to laugh out loud, and the next she nearly hyperventilated in panic.

So many loose ends were swirling in her mind. She still had to go to Washington next week—she was already committed. She'd have to give notice at work, of course, pack up her furniture and ten years of accumulated stuff...

Oh, God. What if none of this worked?

Her heart thudded when the ranch came into view. She took a breath, ordered herself to stay calm, and turned into the driveway. Her tire treads were still spitting stubborn bits of gravel that pinged against the wheel wells. A tractor blocked the way between the two-story ranch house and the horse barn, so she eased the Suburban around and parked in the side yard next to Jack's horse trailer.

Before she could reach for the door handle, her cell phone rang and she nearly jumped out of her skin. She checked the caller ID, then punched the button. "Hey, Stormie."

"You're still a pain in the butt, Pip."

"But you love me anyway. What's up?"

"I checked into Stanley Levin's whereabouts, like you asked. There's nothing funny going on. His girlfriend came into a sizable inheritance and had to be in Tennessee right away to sign papers or the stepsister would inherit by default. I didn't get all the details, but that's pretty much why they packed up and left in a hurry. I talked to Stanley. He and Lucinda are happily living on her family's estate, and they've started their own clinic."

"Well, I'm glad it worked out for him." The man was in love, and she'd been half convinced he might be nuts, somehow responsible for Jack's dead cattle. Now she felt guilty. Had she done the same in regard to Duane? That poor man had lost his wife and child. No wonder Jack had snapped.

"Anything else I can help you out with?"

"Nope. I'm—" She frowned, leaning over to see past the horse trailer. "That's weird."

"What?" Storm asked.

"Hang on." She slid out of the Suburban, left the door ajar and stood by the front fender, where she was still hidden from view by the three-axle trailer. She saw Duane Keegan walk into the feed barn. That wasn't anything out of the ordinary, and his demeanor wasn't at all furtive.

What struck her as odd was the denim jacket he wore. Especially since it was eighty-five degrees out, with ninety percent humidity.

"Listen, I've got to go, Storm. I might be wrong, but to be on the safe side, send a deputy to Jack's ranch. Now.'' She was so nervous she ended the call. In hindsight, as she approached the feed barn, she acknowledged that keeping the line open might have been best.

She eased around the corner of the barn, held her breath, trying to keep her footsteps silent. She needed a moment for her eyes to adjust to the dim interior, which smelled of grain and hay. A forklift sat empty by a neatly stacked row of barrel-shaped hay bales and blocks of salt.

Duane was standing at the waist-high workbench at the opposite end of the barn, his back to her. She felt like a fool. If he was up to no good, he wouldn't be there in clear view of the open doorway. She didn't have the nerve to stroll down the center aisle, so she skirted the wall and stopped ten feet away from the wooden workbench.

Staying hidden between huge bins holding various grains, she watched Duane pinch off a hunk of fodder. Then he reached inside his jacket and pulled out something flat, and Sunny's eyes widened when she saw it snap open into a four-sided box.

My God. A collapsible bucket. She tried to stand still, but it was difficult. He could be on a legitimate mission, something to do with ranch business that she didn't know about—although she was pretty darn knowledgeable when it came to nutrition and an animal's diet.

He dumped the handful of dried grasses into the container, took an opaque, dark-blue bottle from his pocket and poured a liquid substance over the feed. Oh, God, she should have kept Storm on the line. Or run for Jack. But now there wasn't time.

Outrage pumped adrenaline through her veins, yet

five years of self-defense training helped her channel the emotion. That didn't stop the rapid beat of her heart, or the tremors shaking her; it merely gave her the confidence to initiate a confrontation. As she'd told Jack out by the creek, a good aim with a gun wasn't her only asset. But she'd never been forced to test her fighting skills outside of competition or controlled class environments.

On silent feet, she walked up behind Duane. He was so overconfident he hadn't once darted a glance around to see if he was being watched.

"I hope that's a vitamin tonic recommended by the resident veterinarian you're using there."

He didn't even flinch. He turned, leaned casually against the workbench and crossed his arms. "Since you're obviously the resident vet at the moment, seems you'd know that answer."

Although he appeared relaxed, the frigid eyes drilling into her held the frightening stare of madness. This wasn't the quiet, respectful, helpful man she'd worked beside for the past three weeks. This was a man who'd been bucked off one too many rodeo bulls.

"I don't particularly like the answer I'm coming up with," she said. "You really had me stumped, you know? I've been testing for toxic residue in the overall feed supply and troughs. Your eagerness to help takes on new meaning now. You knew I wouldn't find anything."

"Score one for the lady doc." He smirked, and she suddenly realized that aside from probable insanity, this was a man who didn't particularly like women. She'd gone up against his kind more than once.

She made herself relax, tried to edge closer to the

blue bottle to get a better look. He took a step to the side, blocking her move.

"As a professional, I'm really curious how you did this, Duane. If you want to know the truth, I'm actually impressed. I thought I was pretty good, but you've got me and the best lab people in the country beat hands down." She saw the slight change in his expression, the spark of pride and ego.

"I'd never have thought of a collapsible feed bucket," she continued. "But it's perfect. Carry it out into the pasture, pick a cow at random and offer it a snack, and you never leave a trace. Do you use an herbal composition or a pharmaceutical?"

"You might call it a combination of both." He grinned, and she could see he was caught up in his own sick world. "It's amazing what you can buy right over the Internet. Complete with detailed instructions and information on stuff that'll never show up in an autopsy."

She surreptitiously noted her surroundings, imprinted a firm image in her mind of her escape route. She could probably outrun him if need be. A deputy was on his way, or likely Storm himself. She had enough evidence to send Duane to jail. But she couldn't take the chance that his tenuous hold on sanity might break—and lock away the rest of the answers she desperately wanted to know.

"I'm glad to find out we're not dealing with a transmittable disease that could wipe out all the livestock in the valley." She forced an easy smile, felt her eye twitch, hoped like hell he'd confirm her statement.

"Hey, I'm not stupid. I only wanted it to *look* like a contagious disease. I didn't expect it to be so fast-acting, though. Figured there'd be at least a couple of days when the cow would stumble around, cause more of a stir. I already knew it worked fast on humans, but that wasn't an accurate gauge, since the stuff's compounded in doses meant for a thousand-pound animal.''

Sunny swallowed back panic. He'd murdered a human being as well as two animals?

''Why Jack's cows?''

''Because they should have been mine. He stole them from me. Like he stole everything else.''

Her gaze sharpened when he shrugged off his denim jacket and pulled a gun from the waistband of his pants. A deluded psychotic with a thirty-eight-caliber pistol was very likely more than her hand-to-hand defense skills could handle. She could block an assault, but not a bullet.

She held up her hands, took a careful step back. ''Now, let's just calm down here. I'm only a veterinarian. Infectious disease is as far as my jurisdiction or expertise goes. Anything other than that is none of my business, and I don't get involved. The only reason I came in here in the first place was that I saw you and wanted to make sure I had a chance to say goodbye. My vacation time's up and I'm headed home. Only scientific curiosity made me even ask about the pharmaceutical compound.'' She was talking too fast, made herself slow down, concentrate on acting nonchalant.

''If you've got a beef with Jack, I'm the last person who'll stop you. I erased him from my favorite-people list a long time ago when he dumped me for a waitress.''

Instead of pointing the gun at her as she'd expected,

he merely laid it on the workbench. A power play to shake her up? Direct hit.

She followed the movement of his hand. The fraction of relief she felt sent a rush of dizziness to her brain, a distraction she knew better than to allow. If it wasn't for her body's helpless reaction, she would have never made the mistake of taking her eyes off her opponent's.

"I know," Duane said. "Lanette was mine. And she was pregnant with my kid."

JACK YANKED OPEN the front door, every muscle in his body bunched tighter than a catch rope around a steer's neck. Simba bounded out before the door closed, nearly mowing him down, then sat at the edge of the porch and looked back hopefully.

Sunny was still at her mother's and Beau had taken Tori with him to the market, so the dog had made himself at home in Jack's office, sitting politely in the wing chair that faced his desk. Jack hadn't had the heart to make him get down.

He paused and patted Simba's huge head. The dog licked his wrist, his soft brown eyes darting away as though he was suddenly entranced with the puffy flowers on the hydrangea bush by the porch. Silly mutt. A person couldn't help but be crazy about him. He was the size of a small pony, with the heart of a kitten, and not a single aggressive gene beneath that brown coat.

"Well, come on, then." Dog tags jangled as Simba rushed to follow, panting happily as he trotted beside Jack, matching his pace as they headed toward the bunkhouse. "I don't know how the hell you do it. I'm ready to tear somebody's head off and you make me feel guilty. Never thought I'd consider a d—''

Jack stopped, censored his words, remembering the times Sunny had covered her dog's ears, insisting Simba got his feelings hurt easily. The woman flat-out charmed him.

And he honest to God didn't know if he had the strength to let her go. He needed to talk to his brother. Linc was the only one who'd understand the turmoil inside him.

But Jack had something else to deal with first. He wanted to know why Duane Keegan hadn't told him about his involvement with Lanette.

He figured Duane would still be in the bunkhouse, catching a nap before he left to relieve the other men guarding the herd. Maybe Duane had kept quiet about Lanette because he'd worried it might cause hard feelings and jeopardize their friendship. But Sunny's earlier comments, and the telephone conversation he'd just had as a result, sent cold fingers of unease down his spine. Had he been sending the fox to guard the henhouse?

He'd find out soon enough. The bunkhouse was the next building over from the feed barn. He didn't care if Duane had been sleeping with Lanette. He just wanted everything out in the open—especially with this cloud of doom hanging over his ranch.

Simba gave a menacing growl and stopped in his tracks by the entrance to the barn, the fur on his back standing straight up. Jack slid his fingers around the dog's collar. ''What's wrong, boy?''

He looked through the open doors of the barn. Rage consumed him. He wasn't sure if he let go of the dog's collar or if Simba broke free, but a second later both of them were racing forward at a dead run.

Like a dream in slow motion, Jack saw Simba loping down the center aisle of the barn, saw his own boot in midair, one step behind. He heard a roar of outrage—his own—and saw Duane's fist glance off Sunny's cheek, just as the force of Simba's flying leap knocked the man back.

The surreal haze seemed to go on forever, though it couldn't have lasted more than seconds. Part of Jack's brain registered that Sunny was struggling to get up off the ground. Forward momentum and unbridled fury had him driving his fist into Duane's face. Knuckles connected with flesh and bones three times before Simba intervened, shoving them both off balance.

Jack lost his hold. Duane twisted away and grabbed for something on the workbench. Oh, God. A gun. Sunny was on her feet, and Simba, too, both within point-blank range.

Once again time seemed to stand still for endless moments. Jack caught Simba and heaved. Sunny sprang forward, and Jack lunged. Duane's hand closed around the gun. Simba went sliding across the floor....

And God almighty, Sunny was airborne. Her foot connected with Duane's hand before he'd managed even half a revolution. The gun sailed upward toward the hayloft.

Jack slammed his body into Duane's, and they went down hard, limbs tangling in the struggle. He felt his knuckles scrape on the cement. An elbow caught him in the solar plexus. He smelled cinnamon, heard a string of cursing. It wasn't coming from Duane.

"Damn it, Jack. Get that rope by your boot."

It took him a moment to realize Sunny was in the heap, as well, and it was *her* hand pinning Duane's arm at a taut angle that threatened to snap bones.

A fiery haze still colored his vision. The image of Duane's fist hitting Sunny's cheek wouldn't subside.

"I'll take it from here." Rage made his voice deadly quiet. His chest felt like a pressure cooker ready to explode.

"No, you won't." Her voice was just as soft, though not with anger. Over the din of Duane's loud protests, the steady strength of her gaze reached clear to Jack's soul, a whisper of magic that somehow cooled the heat of scorching temper, left him enchanted, entranced and stunned.

He could have killed Duane Keegan with his bare hands. The delayed realization shocked him. He hadn't felt this blindly out of control since the day of his mother's funeral, when his father—still drunk and denying any fault for the deadly accident—had taken a horsewhip to Linc for crying in public.

"The rope?" she prodded, straddling Duane's back as though they were playing a game.

Jack sat up, making sure Duane wouldn't get a jump on her, then reached for the rope, his mind clear, his hands steady. "Well, hell, sugar bear. I was trying to be manly and rescue you."

She plucked the rope out of his hands and had Duane's wrists and ankles tied quicker than any rodeo cowboy Jack had ever seen. It impressed the hell out of him.

"A flea wouldn't need rescuing from this coward," she said in a voice that shook slightly. Adrenaline ebb, Jack realized. His own was still pumping. He stood and helped Sunny to her feet, felt the tremors in her hands, as well. He stroked a thumb over the red mark on her cheek, which would soon turn into a bruise. The urge to beat Duane Keegan to a pulp for touching her clawed for release, but giving in to it wouldn't do either of them any good.

"Are you all right?" he asked.

She nodded. "He's using some kind of poison on the cattle. He claims it's untraceable, but now that we've got the evidence, the lab can match it. I saw him doctoring the feed. And I think he used a human guinea pig to test it out."

Jack bent down and hauled Duane up by his bound wrists, sat him against the wall and ignored the foul language spitting from the man's swollen mouth.

"After you left, I ran across Lanette's death certificate and called the doctor who treated her in the emergency room. He remembered the case because he'd wanted to order an autopsy but couldn't get a signed consent. The boyfriend who brought Lanette in, who turns out to be none other than our trussed-up turkey—" he nodded toward Duane "—insisted she'd want to be cremated, and raised a stink about getting her body released. But my name was listed in her wallet as next of kin, and they notified me."

Duane smirked. "How's it feel to know I had her first, Slade? And last."

Jack hadn't been positive it was Duane. The hospital records noted "Duane Keeley" as the boyfriend who'd filled out the paperwork. Obviously, it hadn't been a coincidence that "Keeley" sounded so similar to "Keegan."

Ignoring the taunt, he leveled his gaze on Duane. "Lanette had the classic symptoms of an overdose, but the toxicology report showed only a small amount of

cocaine in her blood, not enough to cause death. What
do you think tipped the scales, Duane?''

''Ask the dead woman.''

''Oh, I intend to. I'm having her body exhumed and
autopsied. They can do that these days. I'm betting the
medical examiner will find all the evidence he needs
to match the stuff in that bottle over there.''

''Shut up!'' Duane shouted. ''Just shut up. The only
point we have to discuss is my kid. Victoria's mine,
you know. Only a fool couldn't see that. I came home
for a couple of days between rodeos, and when I left
you moved right in on my woman.''

The claim of paternity echoed in Jack's mind, re-
verberating in the ghostly screech of his ex-wife's
voice.

''Everything you've got should be mine,'' Duane
shouted. ''I should be living here. Your old man even
said so.''

''When the two of you were drunk?'' The times
Duane breezed into town and drank himself into a stu-
por with Russell Slade hadn't severed his and Jack's
friendship, but it had created distance. Sober, Duane
had been cool to hang out with. Still, Jack hadn't
known Duane was dating Lanette, and Lanette had
never mentioned it, either.

''You changed the will,'' Duane accused. ''You
stole everything from me and I'll get it back.'' His
voice rose to a childish whine, making it difficult to
understand his ramblings.

''What you're going to get,'' Jack said, ''is a life
sentence for murder. As for Tori, your timing's way
off, pal. She's one hundred percent mine.''

A vehicle skidded to a stop outside, and doors

slammed. Jack glanced over at Sunny. Simba's ears stood at attention, but he didn't budge from her side.

"I was talking on the phone to Storm when I saw Duane come in here," Sunny said. She snapped her fingers at Simba. "Go tell the deputy where we are, boy."

The dog took off like a bullet. Jack was starting to believe that animal *was* part human. A minute later, Storm and two deputies entered, guns drawn. Simba pranced ahead of them proudly.

"Is everything all right?" Storm asked, assessing the scene in a matter of seconds. He holstered his gun and nodded to the deputies to do the same.

"Thanks to your sister's skill with a rope," Jack said. "And her flying feet."

Storm grinned, but his eyes were deadly when he got a good look at Sunny's cheek. "I talked her into taking karate lessons. What are you, Pip? Brown or black belt?"

"Black. Now, do your duty and get this scum out of here."

"What am I charging him with?"

"Suspicion of murder, to start," Jack answered. He didn't fully understand Duane's reasoning, what he'd hoped to accomplish by poisoning Lanette or the cattle. He doubted anyone ever would.

While he and Sunny brought Storm up-to-date, the deputies untied Duane, replaced the ropes with handcuffs and led him out. He was quiet now, his shoulders hunched, reminding Jack of the sad rodeo cowboy who'd shown up a few months back, mourning the loss of his career and his family.

"Stop by the station when you can to give us a formal statement," Storm said, snagging Jack's attention. "And you better call Mama, Pip. If the grapevine gets to her first, I'll never hear the end of it." He headed out, then swore softly and changed directions, moving the heavy wooden door that folded back toward the inside wall. "It's okay, honey. You can come out."

Jack's heart leaped into his throat, a wave of dread engulfing him. Tori was supposed to be in town with Beau. Jack's worst fear was realized when she stepped out from behind the door, tears tracking down her cheeks. My God. How much had she heard?

He reached her in three strides, dropped to his knees and snatched her to his chest. "It's okay, darlin'. Daddy's right here. Everything will be just fine." Sunny knelt at his side, her hand joining his on Tori's narrow back.

"You didn't give me away," Tori whispered, her voice trembling in surprise and fear.

Stunned, he kissed her cheeks and wiped at her tears, his heart shredding. "Of course not. I'd never give away my girl."

"But I'm not your girl." Her brown eyes held a torment no child should harbor.

Without taking his eyes off Tori, he was aware of Beau and Cora racing through the door, skidding to a stop, hovering. Jack's throat ached with emotions he didn't dare let loose. "Why would you say something like that, darlin'?"

"Because I heard you and Mom fighting. I was supposed to be in bed, but I listened at the top of the stairs. You told Mom to be quiet, but she was mean. She said you weren't my daddy." Tori focused on Sunny, her eyes avoiding Jack's, but he held on to her small hands.

"Mom left, but she didn't want me to go with her 'cause she said I was a brat. I was scared, but Daddy didn't make me go away. I thought he was waiting for my mom to come back and get me when she wasn't so mad. Then one day, Daddy left, and when he came home he said Mom went to heaven to live with the angels. I knew what that meant. She wasn't ever coming back. And Daddy wasn't my real daddy. He didn't have to keep me." Tears flowed in a steady stream.

Simba whined and licked Tori's fingers, but the distraught little girl didn't react. "I tried to be extra good so he wouldn't give me away. If I was good, he would still love me, and if the real man came to take me away, Daddy might want to tell him no."

Devastated, unable to listen to another heartbreaking word, Jack folded Tori in his arms again, rocking her. She'd lived with horrible fear and uncertainty all those years. He should have known. Sunny had guessed, had pointed out Tori's reserve around strangers—especially men. His little girl had been terrified a man might someday show up and claim to be her father. And Jack would just hand her over.

Cupping the back of Tori's head, her cheek on his shoulder, he glanced at Sunny, saw the tears on her face and genuine love in her eyes. He didn't know how much one man could bear without crumbling, and right now, Sunny's gaze was his lifeline. *Please help me make this right. I'm bleeding inside. I can't lose both of you.* The plea shouted in his brain but never made it past his lips. He had to do this on his own, could only fight for one love at a time.

And by God, he was going to fight. But Tori came first. He didn't care what it took. He'd make sure from now on that his daughter knew without a doubt she was safe. He didn't need a DNA test to define his love, hadn't cared if Lanette was lying or telling the truth. His feelings had never once wavered.

He eased Tori back, held her small shoulders in his hands. "Look here, darlin'." When he had her attention, he said, "I would never, *ever* let you go. And no one's going to take you from me, either. I promise. You are Victoria Slade. I was in the hospital room when you were born, and I held you before anyone else did. You were so tiny, but you filled up my heart and I loved you from the very first instant you blinked your eyes at me. That will never change."

Tori stared at him with such hope and relief he could hardly get words past the aching lump in his throat. "My name is right there on your birth certificate for anyone who wants to look. It says Jackson Dwight Slade—father. I can put it in the drawer by your bed if you need me to. That way, if you ever get scared or worried, it'll be right there where you can read it. You're my daughter, Tori. My girl." His voice cracked and he desperately battled back his emotions. "You'll always be in my heart."

"Mine, too," Sunny said, and wiped away the last of Tori's tears. She felt Jack go still beside her, but kept her gaze on Tori. "Are you all better now? No more leaky eyes? It's fine by me if you need to cry some more," she added quickly. "I just wondered if I should find a boat and oars in case you flooded the barn."

Tori laughed. "You're so funny." She kissed Sunny on the cheek, whispered, "I know what we talked about, but I love you anyway." Before Sunny could reciprocate, Tori hopped over to Jack and kissed him, too.

The little girl stood back and stared at them both with utter trust and acceptance. Children gave their hearts so easily.

Sunny saw Jack's Adam's apple bob several times. She was so touched by the man he had become—the man he'd always been, she saw clearly now. When he loved, he did it unconditionally—and forever.

Simba worked his head under Tori's hand, and she scratched his ears. "Duane's not coming back, is he, Daddy?"

"Never," Jack answered. "That's a promise, darlin'."

"Good." She looped her arm over Simba's neck, giggled when he licked her face. Beau and Cora were still standing just inside the open door, holding on to each other as though neither had the strength to stand alone.

"Sweetie, would you do me a favor?" Sunny asked. "Simba's trying his best to pretend he's not upset, but I can tell he is." Simba dutifully lowered his ears, and Tori hugged his neck, crooned to him not to be sad. "Maybe you could take him in the house with Beau and Cora."

Beau gave a discreet sniff. "I've got a big T-bone I bet he'd like."

"And I've got brownies," Cora added, quickly mopping her face with Beau's bandanna.

"He can't have any chocolate," Tori announced, then looked back at Sunny. "Are you and Daddy coming in pretty soon?"

"We'll be there in just a few minutes."

Tori's gaze skittered away. "You don't have to be that quick. Stay a long time if you want." Then she raced out the door, with Beau and Cora trying to keep up.

Jack chuckled. "If I know my daughter, she's counting on getting a head start on the brownies— without me there to monitor the sugar grams."

Sunny had planned to reveal her feelings in stages, but her heart simply overflowed. "I've never loved a man more than I do you right this minute."

He went abruptly, absolutely still. Sunny swallowed, her heart nearly pounding out of her chest. "I know the timing's awful," she said, "after what we've all just been through, but I have to ask. Do you love me?"

"Sunny—"

"Just answer the question. Please."

"More than I could ever express."

A scream of frustration built like a gathering thunderhead. She didn't know whether to laugh with joy or clobber him. "Obviously," she snapped, "since you *haven't* expressed it."

"I didn't want to pressure you. Especially after you told me about feeling manipulated by people in your life."

"Manip— I was merely sharing a personal revelation! Telling you something I'd recognized about myself and had decided not to tolerate anymore." She should definitely clobber him, she decided. Maybe it would knock some sense into him.

"Honestly, Jack, if you're going to live in a house full of women, you better get a clue that most females are a work in progress. We devour self-help books and tape talk shows so we don't miss a subject that might apply to us. If something's bugging us, one of those venues is going to reach out and zap us in the butt, and we'll blaze ahead and fix the problem. I did that. It's done. I've moved on. And even though it no longer applies, did it ever occur to you that *you* were being manipulative by developing lockjaw? Deciding what kind of pressure was good or bad for me?"

"No—"

"Well, from now on, damn it, say what you mean and mean what you say—"

He hauled her against his chest, his eyes blazing with amusement, love and endearing masculine confusion.

"I love you, Sunny Leigh Carmichael. I have no idea what all you just said, but I do know, without a doubt, that I love you." Then he lowered his head and kissed her until she couldn't think straight. When he relinquished her lips at last, they were both breathing like Thoroughbreds after a race.

"Did that tell you I mean what I say?" he asked.

"Um…yes. Very nicely, thank you."

He laughed at her prim response, then groaned and touched his forehead to hers. "I hope you know I can't let you go now."

"I was sort of counting on you feeling that way."

"I've always felt that way, sweetheart. You're the only woman I've ever loved. I still need to clear it with Linc, but I'm going to put this place up for sale and buy us a ranch in California. Someone told me you can't beat the weather there. And I've always had a hankering to try my hand at surfing."

Sunny's heart melted. This land was his soul, but he'd give it up for her. "I don't know why you'd want to buy a ranch in California when my business and all my family and friends are here in Hope Valley."

"What are you saying?"

"That I love you, Jack Slade. I always have and I always will. I want to be Tori's mother and have more babies with you. And since the town appears to be without a vet, I intend to take the position and go back into private practice, where my heart truly is. There are plenty of cows and horses to keep me busy, and the poodles and rabbits will provide a nice variety. I love Tori to pieces, but I'm drawing the line at tending snakes. Including Gordie."

Jack laughed, picked her up and swung her around. She was so special, this petite veterinarian who hog-tied bad guys, bossed around cattle ten times her size, talked to a goofy dog as though he were a person, and could be taken down by an innocent garter snake. She was a woman full of surprises.

And the absolute love of his life.

"Will you marry me, sweetheart?"

Sunny wrapped her arms tight around his neck, kissed him for all the years they'd missed and all the ones to come.

"I thought you'd never ask," she said against his mouth. "Suppose we should go tell the rest of the family?"

"They'd appreciate the news. Unless you want to get a jump on the honeymoon and take advantage of these hay bales."

"We've been caught with our pants down in the hay before. Perhaps we should exercise a bit more decorum in our advanced age." She thought about it for all of two seconds. "To heck with decorum. Lock the barn doors, cowboy."

Jack didn't waste any time. Sunny was back in

Texas to stay, in his arms and in his life. They had a second chance, and this time was forever. Because Sunny Carmichael always had been, and always would be, the other half of his soul.

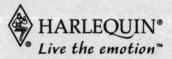

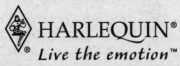

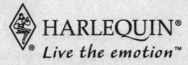

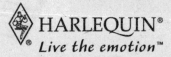